Viking Myths

Stories of the Norse Gods and Goddesses

Viking Myths

Stories of the Norse Gods and Goddesses

retold by Thor Ewing

with illustrations by the author

WELKIN BOOKS

First Published 2014
Welkin Books Ltd

ISBN 978-1-910075-00-5

...vesa munu bǫnd í landi ...

— *Stefnis þáttr Þorgilssonar*

Acknowledgements

I'd like to thank all the children and adults who have listened to these stories over the years, my father who first introduced me to Viking stories, and my wife and family for their continuing patience. A special mention should also go to my wife's uncle David Schutte, whose encouragement began the long process of turning the stories in my head into the book in your hand.

Also to all those who have read the early drafts of the book and added their comments, in particular to my mother and brother, to my wife, to Jane Lawrence, to Charlotte Bulley, and to Laura and Ben Tarlo Ross.

Finally, I'd also like to mention my wonderful primary school teacher Mr Robert Stern, who did so much to foster my interest in myth, history and literature.

Contents

Introduction   10

A Note about the Pictures   21

1. Beginnings   25

2. Nine Worlds and Mimir's Wood   31

3. The Aesir   37

4. The First of Wars   44

5. Niord's Children   50

6. The Apples of Life   59

7. Loki's Children   70

8. Loki's Wager   76

9. Thor the Bride   85

10. The Builder's Fee   92

11. Thor's Trip to Outgarth   99

12. Games in Outgarth   109

13. Aegir's Brewpot   119

14. The Fight with Hrungnir   131

15. Peace with Geirrod   140

16. Balder's Death   147

17. Loki's Bickering   157

18. Loki's Binding   164

19. Kvasir's Blood   170

20. Bale Work   175

21. The Doom of the Powers   184

Index of Names   193

Introduction

The Viking myths are a delight for everyone who has ever lost themselves in a world of stories. They can help us understand how the Vikings saw their world, as well as their gods and religion. But they are also wonderful stories in their own right, which can still hold lessons for us today.

For me, these stories have a special significance. I first heard many of them from my father when I was a boy, and since then I've been telling and retelling the myths to audiences up and down the country, and even taking them back across the sea to Scandinavia. So although the original Viking storytellers lived a thousand years ago, I feel very much a part of this ancient storytelling tradition.

The Viking myths have an amazing power to captivate listeners. Sharing these stories with a wide variety of audiences, adults and children, has been a wonderful opportunity for me to shape my own retelling of these timeless myths. I want to be sure that the stories you read here should be true to the spirit of the original storytellers. So in each case, I have gone right back to the original source, to check every detail against the definitive ancient version.

What is myth?

Not everyone agrees about the dividing lines between the different genres of Myth, Legend and Folk Tale. But for me, the difference lies in two questions: 'Who is it about?' and 'When is it set?'

If it's a Myth, then the main protagonists are gods or otherworldly beings, and the story is set in a timeless arena that stands outside history. The story of the theft of Thor's hammer for instance, is narrated as something which happened long ago but it bears no relation to human history, and the myth might also have a seasonal meaning in our own time representing the disappearance of thunder in wintertime.

In a Legend, on the other hand, the main protagonists are named human heroes who are said to have lived in a specific historical era and to have taken part in (and often helped to shape) its major events.

The main protagonists in a Folk Tale or Fable are often nameless, or else have very commonplace or ridiculous names; the stories are set in an unspecific, ahistorical past, and could take place against more-or-less any historical backdrop.

In some tales gods and people might play equal parts, but these can usually be categorised as either Legends or Folk Tales.

However, although these categories seem pleasingly sharp, it can sometimes be a short step from one form to another. Medieval writers tried to set the myths in pseudo-historical contexts, recasting the gods as human heroes. In so doing, they transformed ancient myths into medieval legends, and it is not always possible to say where one form ends and another begins.

Gods, truth and myth

For us the word 'myth' has a double meaning. On the one hand a myth can be a story about ancient gods, and on the other it can represent any untruth which is widely believed. So did the Vikings really believe their 'myths' in the same way that for instance, some people insist on the belief that the Earth is flat?

Nowadays, we tend to see the gods simply as fictional characters inhabiting a colourful world of stories. But for the mythmakers, it was quite different. If we want to understand their myths, we should try to see things from their point of view.

For them, the gods represented aspects of reality cloaked in human form: Roughly speaking, we may say that Thor is the thunderstorm (which is the most tangible sign of a hidden energy underpinning our existence); Odin is fury, prophecy and other forms of inspiration; Freya is desire, and her brother Frey is growth and wealth. Their enemies can be seen as the harsher forces of frost and ice, bleak mountains and barren wastes.

Myths are a way to explore the relationship between these divine forces through storytelling, and there was probably never one single version of any given myth. Because there were already many ways to tell the story, every storyteller could retell each tale in his own way. This process of change and creativity which seems to lie behind the myths, along with the playfulness with which the myths express their underlying ideas, suggests that even if some folk might have believed every word, there were always people canny enough to see the myths as wonderful metaphors rather than as literal history.

Morality and the myths

If you're expecting fairy tales with good heroes and bad villains, you might sometimes find these stories an uncomfortable read. The myths don't tell us how to be good and so, unlike in fairy stories, goodness is not always rewarded. This doesn't mean the Vikings didn't value goodness, gentleness and kindness - indeed everyone loves Balder for these very qualities. The Viking gods are on the side of right; it's just that they don't always play fair.

This moral ambiguity is an inevitable consequence of the nature of the gods. For the early mythmakers, the gods and their enemies were not simply characters in a story, but natural forces locked in a real struggle. Such forces are not easily constrained by the niceties of human convention. Yet although the myths might often be morally ambiguous, they are far from amoral. In fact, they are profoundly interested in moral questions, even if they consistently refuse easy answers.

What is more, we ourselves are implicated in the moral failings of the gods. They might often seem unfair and unjust, but they are on our side and our own lives are dependent on the forces they represent. In the myths, it is sometimes only by cheating or lying that the gods manage to survive at all. Uncomfortable as it might make us feel, we know we should be rooting for our side no matter what means they use to achieve their ends.

As humans, we might know that we are on the side of the gods, but our side rarely succeeds in taking the moral high ground. Instead, through the prism of myths, we watch our champions and protectors desperately struggling by fair means or foul to maintain their hold over the world. Lacking the comfort of a single all-powerful God as the unquestionable source of morality for his Creation, the Vikings looked up to a few personified characteristics to hold back the tide of entropy and chaos. For them, the realm of the gods was not make-believe, but a parallel reality that helps us to make sense of our own. So despite their apparently fantastical nature, the purpose of the myths is not to show us how the world should be, but to describe it as it is.

In this retelling

I wanted to preserve this moral ambiguity and not try to hide it. Ever since Annie and Eliza Keary's aptly-named classic *The Heroes of Asgard* was published in 1857, modern retellings have tended to read as propaganda for the Aesir, but the oldest versions are rather more even-handed.

I also wanted to avoid the solemn and ponderous style which has bedevilled some retellings. Instead, I have tried to restore something of the freshness and vitality of the oldest versions, which have a plain-spoken elegance sometimes rising to an austere poetic beauty.

I believe that myths are not designed for any one particular age group; it is a form of story for adults and children alike. So my book is for everyone, and I hope that it is enjoyable and accessible for readers of all ages, young and old alike.

The Norse myths are chock-full of names. Every horse, every house, even the occasional domestic utensil has its own name. Some readers struggle with all these foreign-looking names, while other readers are seduced by the exotic glamour they lend to the myths. Either way they get between the reader and the story. To short-circuit this, I have often opted to translate the meaning of Norse names. These translations aren't always completely literal, but they take us closer to the spirit of the original tales, and away from the mystique of foreign names. The original Norse forms (sometimes with more literal English renderings) can be found in the Index at the back of the book.

On the other hand, I have abandoned the usual translation of the Norse words *jǫtunn* and *þurs* as 'giant'. It is true that some of the *jǫtnar* are giant-sized, but others seem to be no bigger than anyone else. And our notion of the storybook giant is not always appropriate to these cunning elemental opponents of gods and men. Instead I have used the old Scots word 'etin', which is cognate with the Norse *jǫtunn*. This word may be familiar to readers through the folktale 'The Red Etin of Ireland' and the old ballad of 'Hind Etin'.

Editorial considerations

I have tried to give a sense not just of the individual stories but of the whole system of the mythology leading from creation to ultimate destruction. Each myth stands alone as a tale in its own right but, although they don't always sit completely comfortably alongside their immediate neighbours, most do slot more-or-less happily into the overall framework, suggesting that many must have had a fixed place in the sequence even before they were first written down.

A certain amount of reshaping is still inevitable, but while early storytellers might have had a free hand to interpret the myths however they wanted, we can't be quite so easy-going today. If we take too many liberties with these stories, they're no longer Viking myths but modern myths. Perhaps lost originals might once have told a different story, but the tales that survive in our earliest sources must always remain the definitive account for this and all future retellings.

The Viking myths survive in various sources. Some are told in *Snorra Edda*, a handbook of poetics written by the thirteenth-century Icelander, Snorri Sturluson. Others are told in narrative poems composed towards the end of the Viking Age. Others still, which are not explicitly told in any one surviving source, can be drawn out of scattered references in several sources.

Snorri undoubtedly gives us our most complete overall picture of Viking mythology, but his versions of the myths are usually told in the briefest possible manner, and he often skips the parts he doesn't need. The outstanding exception is the story of Thor's adventure in Outgarth, which he tells at greater length than I have done here (Chapters 11 & 12, 'Thor's Trip to Outgarth' and 'Games in Outgarth').

Snorri wrote another very different version of some of the myths in his *Ynglinga saga*, where they are woven into the story of the ancient kings of Norway. Between them, these two early versions show how much a single storyteller was able to change his story to meet his needs. Not many years before Snorri set down his stories in Iceland, a Dane called Saxo also recorded several myths in his monumental *Gesta Danorum*, a Latin history of the Danish people. For him, the stories of the gods were woven into ancient history, but his account can still sometimes shed vital light on what we glean from other sources.

As I have said above, where there is more than one account of any myth, they invariably disagree. So, a modern retelling has to find the path that seems best to represent the surviving traditions. Some myths on the other hand have only survived in broken fragments, which have to be put carefully back together. With so many gaps and contradictions, we are forced to use logic and ingenuity to make a coherent tapestry out of the surviving fragments.

This is a storybook, and the plot choices I have made here are first and foremost the choices of the storyteller, but since these are Viking stories rather than my own, I have always been guided by scholarship and by hints in the original texts. Sometimes I have been able to 'reconstruct' lost passages by triangulating between surviving sources; at other times the forces of narrative logic and knowledge of the culture have dictated a necessary path. I have briefly explained some of the more significant adaptations below.

I have understood Mimir to be Odin's maternal uncle (Chapter 2, 'Nine Worlds and Mimir's Wood'). Although nowhere explicitly stated, this is consistent with the poem *Hávamál* (st.140) where Odin states that he gained drink and wisdom from 'Bolthor's famous son'; Bolthor is the father of Odin's mother Bestla. In Snorri's version of this myth, Odin travels to meet Mimir and pays with his eye to drink the water from the Well of Wisdom.

In the same group of verses (*Hávamál*, st.138-46), Odin 'takes up' the runes, which he finds in 'the depths' beneath the 'windy tree'. This poem apparently envisages Odin as 'hanging' in the tree, and at the same time able to move freely throughout the tree. In the poem *Vǫluspá* (st.20), the Norns (who are associated with *Urðarbrunnr*, 'Being's Well', beneath the tree) are said to 'cut on wood', making laws and allotting lives to people; this would seem to be the reason the runes are found among the roots of the tree.

In the Old English 'Nine Herbs Charm', Woden (the Anglo-Saxon equivalent of Odin) takes 'nine glory twigs' to attack a serpent; although these 'glory twigs' may be identical with the nine herbs listed in the charm, there are also reasons to associate them with rune sticks. A straightforward reading of the poem suggests that Woden is 'hanging in heaven' when he shapes nine herbs to counteract the contagions caused by the nine serpents. These mythical Anglo-Saxon serpents are very much like the snakes and streams of the Norse *Hvergelmir* ('Seether') in that both are the source of poison and disease in our own world, and there is little doubt in my mind that this is essentially the same myth.

Although different sources might reflect variant (and possibly contradictory) traditions, it seems certain that each of these fragmentary myths would once have been understood within a coherent narrative. I have assimilated these broken shards from disparate sources into one integrated story. We may never know how well this 'retelling' correlates with the lost traditions behind our sources, but by presenting the mythical details as a single coherent myth and using only minimal narrative bridges to link the surviving details, we come closer to the experience of these elements in their proper context than we can get through simply confronting the raw confusion of the extant sources.

The story of Loki's arrival in Asgarth, which is told here in Chapter 3, 'The Aesir', is referred to in the Viking poem *Lokasenna* where significant details are revealed, but it is never explicitly narrated in surviving sources. Other features are suggested with reference to the behaviour of the gods elsewhere in the myths.

In Chapter 6, 'The Apples of Life', I have taken Idun to be the etin Thiassi's sister. According to the late poem *Hrafnagaldr* (st.6), her father was Ivaldi, and Thiassi's father is named as either Alvaldi or Qlvaldi (*Hárbarðsljóð* st.19, *Skáldskaparmál* 42). Although these two figures might not necessarily be seen as identical, the poem *Lokasenna* (rendered here as Chapter 17, 'Loki's Bickering') accuses Idun of embracing her brother's killer. In surviving myths and in all poetic references, Idun is only ever linked with Bragi. Bragi himself seems only to have been involved in a single killing, that of Thiassi who had stolen his wife. Taken together, these details strongly suggest that Thiassi and Idun might originally have been seen as brother and sister.

In Chapter 19, 'Kvasir's Blood', I have substituted the name Billing where most versions have Gilling. The character of Gilling, who appears only in *Snorra Edda*, may result from a misreading of the name Billing. Snorri himself cites a verse by Orm Steinthorsson (*Skáldskaparmál* 47), which refers to Kvasir's blood as 'the drink of Billing's son.' If Gilling and Billing are one and the same, then Billing's son would be Suttung, who took the mead from the dwarfs; otherwise the kenning remains obscure.

Billing's unnamed daughter appears in *Hávamál* (st.96-102), where Odin twice fails to seduce her. This passage comes immediately before the verses describing Odin's theft of the mead from Gunnlod (st.103-110). It is possible that Billing's daughter is identical with Rindr, the mother of Vali. Saxo tells a euhemerised version of her story, making Rinda a princess of the Rus (or 'Ruthenians'), who twice refuses Odin's advances before he disguises himself as a sorceress (Saxo, *Gesta III*). The tenth-century poet Kormákr clearly knew some similar story when he notes that 'Odin used magic on Rindr.' The birth of Vali the Avenger is an important element in the last act of Viking mythology, so putting these accounts together I have come up with the version told here.

Conclusion

The Viking myths have spoken to generations of readers and audiences for more than a thousand years. As well as telling us something about the mindset of our Viking forebears, they can also teach us about ourselves and about the world we live in. But above all, they are great stories.

As stories, they have at least another thousand years of life in them yet, and one day I believe the Viking myths will be just as widely known as the myths of the Classical world.

A Note about the Pictures

We know from Viking literature that myths could be depicted in illustrations. Two 'shield poems' survive, describing mythological pictures decorating splendid shields, and a similar poem describes mythological carvings in an Icelandic hall. There are some surviving images from across the Viking world but unfortunately, almost all this mythological art has been lost. Most was probably painted on shields, woven in tapestries or carved in wood, whereas surviving art is almost entirely in stone and metal.

I wanted the pictures in this book to show how these lost Viking depictions might once have looked. As with the stories themselves, I hope the style used for the illustrations reflects something of the attitudes and beliefs of the original mythmakers. Viking artists seem deliberately to have rejected realistic and naturalistic portrayals of the human form, and this is perhaps especially true in the case of representations of the gods. Early Germanic religious idols were roughly hewn from unshaped logs, even though artists of the time were also capable of beautiful craftsmanship; miniature idols from the later Viking Age are not always quite so crudely made but still reflect a basically similar attitude.

There are very many styles of Viking art, but for this project I was drawn to the simple purposeful style used by stone carvers in Uppland and more especially on the island of Gotland. The art on these 'picture stones' seems to fulfil a similar function to the narrative art described in the shield poems, and there are similarities with fragments of narrative art from elsewhere in the Viking world. So, although it now mainly survives on one Baltic island, the art of the Gotland picture stones might well reflect a more universal Viking style. Also, because the Gotland stones often preserve only the bare outlines of the original images, we need to compare them with a wide range Viking art to understand how the style worked in practice.

Having sketched the lines of the figures in this style, I needed to adapt them to the medium I was working with. Unlike the Viking artists who were carving their work into wood or stone, my illustrations were to be printed on the flat pages of a book. The illusion of solidity had to be drawn into the pictures themselves. So, the illustrations in this book are not meant as a careful exercise in historical authenticity but, rather like the retellings of the stories themselves, as a deliberate adaptation of a Viking style for the modern world.

Beginnings

Before the beginning, there was the Gap. A magical gap, a holy gap called Ginnunga Gap. To the south of Ginnunga Gap burned the fire of Muspell and to the north was the ice of Sleet Waves.

Between them lay the Gap.

Poison welled up from the ice of Sleet Waves and flowed in streams into Ginnunga Gap, where it froze into rivers of ice. There were freezing mists hanging over the ice, and they covered it with layers of frost. The frost and the ice grew ever deeper, until they filled the northmost edge of Ginnunga Gap.

But just as the north of Ginnunga Gap grew heavy with ice and thick with freezing mists, so the south was warmed by the fires of Muspell where the sparks and molten drops flew out across the emptiness towards Sleet Waves. And where the warm wind of Muspell touched the ice of Sleet Waves, the ice was dripping with droplets of water.

These flowing drops took life from the heat of Muspell, and they took on the shape of a huge man. This giant was the etin Ymir, the first living being. He lay sleeping on the ice with his arms outstretched on either side of him. His legs were crossed and his feet together.

As Ymir slept he sweated, and children were born from his flowing sweat. Under one hand there grew a boy, and under the other a girl. Another boy grew between his two feet, but the boy who was born from Ymir's feet had six heads. These were Ymir's children, and they were the first of the etins. From these first etins came more etins, and from more there came yet more.

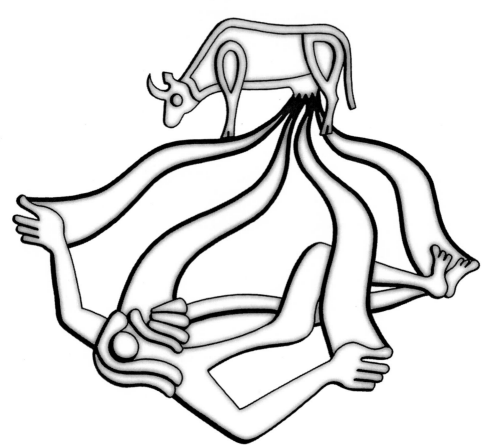

As the ice melted, some of the drops took the shape of a cow. The cow's name was Audhumla. She licked at the ice with her warm tongue, and she lived on the water and the salts that were in the ice. Four streams of milk flowed from Audhumla's udders, which fed Ymir and his children.

Audhumla licked away at the ice, and one day she licked out the shape of a man's hair. The next day she licked out the shape of his head. On the third day, the whole man was there. Then Buri stepped out of the ice. He was beautiful to look at, big and strong.

Buri had a son called Bor, and Bor chose himself a wife called Bestla, who was the daughter of the etin Bolthor. Bestla had three sons with Bor, and their names are Odin and Vili and Ve. They were the first of the gods.

But always there were more etins, and still Ymir lay wallowing over the whole of Sleet Waves, guzzling on Audhumla's milk. The gods looked at the growing tribe of etins, and at their senseless father lying stretched across the ice.

'Ymir sprawls on the ice,' said Odin, 'while bits of his body spawn many-headed monsters. How should this lout be the first of beings and the father of everything? Far better that we seize this chance, and make ourselves the fathers of everything!'

There was a quarrel then between the gods and etins, so that Bor's sons stabbed Ymir to the heart and killed him. And the blood that welled out of Ymir's wounds swept over Sleet Waves, and it washed away the whole race of etins and drowned them.

But there was one etin called Bergelmir, who had made himself a boat. Bergelmir sailed off with his family in his boat, so all etins now are descended from him.

Then the gods took the body of Ymir and carried it to the middle of Ginnunga Gap, and from his flesh they made the earth and all its lands. Out of the blood that flowed freely from his wounds, they made the seas and lakes. And the hairs that grew on Ymir's body became flowers, grasses and trees. The bones inside his body became the rocks beneath the earth. And the gods scattered his teeth across the land as stones and boulders.

Then they took Ymir's skull and set it over everything to make the sky. They put a dwarf at each corner to hold it up, and the names of the dwarfs are North and South, East and West. They took Ymir's brains and scattered them across the sky, and from these they made the clouds.

The gods made a shining bridge of many colours that leads from the earth up into the skies. It is called Bifrost, and it is the strongest and most beautiful of bridges. Its colours are reds and golds and blues, and it is also called the Rainbow. The blue is drawn from the ice of Sleet Waves, but the red that you see in Bifrost is burning fire from Muspell, and not everyone can cross it because of the fire there.

There were hot sparks and molten droplets flying out from Muspell, and the gods set them in the sky as the stars. They chose the brightest two sparks to make the Sun and the Moon as lights for the world.

There was a man called Time Farer who had two children, a boy and a girl. He thought they were the loveliest things in all the world, and so he called the girl 'Sun', and the boy he called 'Moon'.

But the gods were angry with him for this, because he thought as much of his own children as of the Sun and the Moon.

They took the girl whose name was Sun, and they made her drive the wagon of the Sun that is drawn by the two horses Early Waker and All Swift. Her brother, whose name is Moon, they made drive the wagon of the Moon.

These two wagons are always rushing through the skies without stopping to rest, because there are two wolves hunting them down. There's a wolf called Scorn that is chasing the Sun, and a wolf called Hate that chases the Moon. They chase them for ever around the skies, and the Sun and the Moon are running away.

Those wolves were born in the Ironwood of Etinhome. There's another wolf there called Moongarm, who is growing ever bigger on the blood of everyone who dies. And the time will come that he will swallow the Moon and the stars, and he will spatter the skies with blood.

Nine Worlds and Mimir's Wood

This is how the Nine Worlds are set up: The world of the gods is the stronghold of Asgarth; there they made their home, and there they have built fine halls. Our world lies within the walls of Midgarth, which the wise gods made from the etin Ymir's eyelashes. Beyond the outer seas lies the world of Etinhome, which is where the frost etins live, and all sorts of trolls and monsters; it is a world of ice floes, rocks and mountains, and it's very bleak.

Above and below each of these three worlds, there are other worlds in the skies and under the earth, and together these make up the whole of the Nine Worlds.

There is a tree which grows through all these worlds, so that the same tree stands in Midgarth, in Asgarth and in Etinhome. It is known as Yggdrasil, as Odin's Steed, and as Mimir's Wood. Its branches spread across the worlds and reach right up to heaven.

It was on this tree that Odin hanged himself. With a spear in his side, he hung in the branches without food and without drink.

For nine days and nine nights, he was hanging in the sky where the branches of the tree grow up among the stars. But while his body was dead, his mind blew like the breeze through the branches of that tree and throughout every world, so that nothing was hidden from him.

He found there were birds and animals among the branches. Four stags are forever chewing on the leaves and twigs of the tree, and a little squirrel scurries up and down the trunk. The squirrel's name is Rattletusk, and he runs up until he comes to the top of the tree, where there is an eagle called Wide Open. There is a hawk sitting between the eagle's eyes, and the hawk is called Windblown.

Down at the foot of the tree, Odin followed one of the roots deep under Asgarth, where it dips into the clear waters of the Well of Being. Two birds feed in that well, and their feathers are pure white; they are called swans, and all the many swans of Midgarth have come from these two.

That well is tended by three women, who have a beautiful hall there by the well-side. Their names are

Being, Becoming and Necessity, and they are the three Norns. They take water from the well every day and mix it with the white clay that lies around the well, and they pour it up over the wood of the tree so that its branches will never rot or die.

The Norns allot life and death to everyone who has ever lived or is yet to be born. They carve their judgement in rune letters onto the twigs of the tree. Those runes govern everything that will happen in all worlds.

Then Odin grasped the runes. He knew how to cut the runes and how to colour them; he knew how to use the runes and how to wield them.

Another root runs beneath Midgarth into Shadow Home, where there is a well called Seether. It is there that the rivers of Sleet Waves have their source. There was a great snake in that well called Spite Cutter, and it chewed on the root of the tree. Venom seeped up through the root from where Spite Cutter was chewing, spreading rot and sickness throughout the tree.

Spite Cutter was the sworn enemy of the eagle Wide Open at the top of the tree. Every day, the squirrel Rattletusk scurried busily up and down the trunk carrying spiteful words between them, and that's how they came to hate each other although they could never meet.

Odin took nine rune twigs, and he struck the snake so that it flew into nine pieces. But each piece became a living snake so that where before there had been only one snake, now there were nine.

These snakes writhed in the well and started to gnaw at the root of the tree, and there are nine poisons and nine sicknesses that flow from them bringing death into the world. They are gnawing still at the root of the tree, but their sicknesses and their poisons are ruled by the runes and the healing herbs which Odin has shaped against them.

A third root goes deep under Etinhome, and dips into the Well of Wisdom. Odin followed that root down to the well where the aged etin Mimir sat, his mother's brother. Every day, Mimir drank water from the well at the root tip, and he was the wisest of etins.

Odin asked Mimir for a drink of water from the well. But the etin said, 'The water of this well is worth more to me than anything else. You may only taste this water, if you give me whatever is worth most to you.'

So Odin reached into his own head and plucked out his right eye, and he gave that to Mimir. Then Mimir took a horn, dipped it in the water and handed it to Odin.

Odin drank, and with that drink he gained the wisdom of all the worlds.

After nine days and nine nights, Odin's mind came back into his body, and his body came to life again on the tree. He brought the runes back with him; he carved them and coloured them, and he taught them to the gods. And he had the wisdom of Mimir's Well, so that he is now the wisest of gods and there is nothing that is hidden from him.

But since that time, Odin has had only one eye.

The Aesir

Odin is the father of all the gods. His family is called the Aesir, and Asgarth is named after them. Because of this, and because the Nine Worlds and everything in them were shaped by him, Odin is known as All Father. He is also called 'Blind' and 'Hooded', 'Horror' and 'Greybeard'.

Odin's home is called Kill Hall or Valhalla.

Kill Hall is filled with warriors who have been killed in battle, and every day there are more of them. They are called the Lone Warriors, and they train ceaselessly for the Doom of the Powers, when they will fight together against the etins.

There are also women in Odin's hall who are called Kill Choosers or valkyries, and they choose the men who will be killed in battle to join the Lone Warriors. They serve the Lone Warriors there with golden mead which flows from the udders of the goat Bright Secret. And they bring them the meat of the pig Sea Sooty, which is cooked every evening by On Sooty in the pot called Fire Sooty.

Odin does not eat, but gives his food to his two wolves, Greed and Hunger, and he only drinks wine. There are two ravens that sit on his shoulders. Their names are Thought and Memory. They fly out from Asgarth every day, and bring him news from the Nine Worlds.

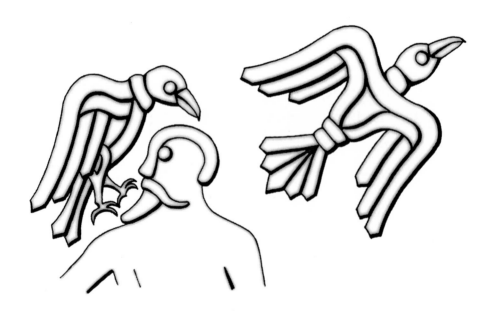

Thor is the first of Odin's sons, and his mother is Earth. He is the biggest and strongest of the gods, with a big red beard and fierce eyes. He has a belt of strength, and iron gloves for his hands. Thor is sometimes called 'Storm Rider'. He rides through the skies in his wagon drawn by the two goats Tooth Gnasher and Tooth Grinder. The rumble of his wagon wheels sounds around the skies, and we hear that sound as thunder.

Thor's hall in Strength Field is the biggest of houses. It is called Thunder Flash, and it has five hundred and forty rooms. Thor lives there with his wife Sif and his followers.

Odin's second son is called Balder. He is so beautiful that light shines from him wherever he goes. He is the wisest and kindest of gods. His voice is soft, and all his judgements are fair and kind-hearted, but not one of them has ever been acted on. Balder's wife is called Nanna, and they live together in the hall called Broad Gleam. It is the most beautiful of houses, and there is nothing there that is evil or unclean.

Balder's mother is Frigg. She is Odin's wife, and she has her home at Fen Hall. There her maidservant Fulla tends to her, and looks after her shoes and her coffers. Frigg is also called Hlin, and she comes to help people in need. Frigg's messenger is Gna, and she rides on her horse Hoof Thrower wherever Frigg sends her throughout the Nine Worlds.

Heimdal has his hall at Heaven Cliff beside Bifrost Bridge at the edge of the skies. He can see for a hundred miles, and he sees as well by night as by day. From his house high up on the Rainbow, Heimdal can see the blades of grass growing in the fields below, and he can hear the bees leaving their hives in the mornings. He needs less sleep than a bird, and he waits and watches for the time when the gods will be attacked in Asgarth.

Then the sons of Muspell will storm over Bifrost, and Heimdal will blow the horn called Yeller Horn to summon the gods and the Lone Warriors to battle for the Doom of the Powers.

In the middle of Asgarth is Ida Field, where long ago the gods would meet among the green grass to play with their golden chessmen. Now it is where they have their Seats of Judgement, where they settle between them what will happen. Lid Shelf is the name of Odin's seat, from where he looks out over all the upper worlds.

The gods have built a hall there for these seats, and it is called Bright Home. It is the best building that stands on earth, and it shines inside and out with pure gold. From there the gods rule over the world.

It was in Bright Home that the Aesir made judgements about the Sun, Moon and stars. They ruled that the Sun should rise in the east every day and go down in the west, and that the stars should turn around the Pole Star in the sky. And they ruled that the Moon should wax and wane in the sky every month.

It was there too that they judged the place of the dwarfs. These had first grown as maggots in Ymir's flesh, but by the judgement of the Aesir they became dwarfs, with sense and understanding and the shape of men. They live now in the earth and rocks, and in Black Elfhome which lies deep under Asgarth.

There was an etin called Hard Beater, and his wife was called Needle or Leafy. They had three sons, whose names were Bee Leg, Hel Blind and Loki. Loki was the youngest. He was clever, quick-witted and handsome, and not much like the rest of his family. In time, Loki set out from Etinhome to join the gods in Asgarth.

When he came to Asgarth, he went in to Bright Home and he walked down the length of the hall, until he stood in front of Odin's high seat of Lid Shelf.

Thor said, 'Who is this youth that has come to our hall? What does he want, and what is there he can do?'

'My name is Loki, son of Leafy,' said the stranger, 'and I have come from Etinhome to join you here.'

Heimdal said, 'No one may join the gods in Asgarth, unless he is the master of some craft. We have all the skills that we need, so there is no place for newcomers here.'

But Odin turned to Loki and said, 'Welcome, Loki, son of Leafy. Each of us here has his own art or skill that fits him for his place among us. What is there that you can do?'

'There is not much that is beyond me,' said Loki, 'and I'll be happy to do whatever you think best.'

The gods found that Loki was full of artful words and quick answers, and he had shoes that could run over sea

and sky. They made judgement that he should be their errand boy, and carry messages for them around the Nine Worlds. Only Heimdal spoke against this judgement.

Then Odin made a cut on his arm and let the blood flow onto the earth, and Loki did the same.

'Loki,' said Odin, 'you were not born as one of the Aesir, but now our blood is mixed in the earth and you belong with us as our brother. No food shall be served among us and no beer shall be poured, unless it is shared with you.'

So Loki became one of the Aesir, and took his place at the Seats of Judgement on Ida Field.

The First of Wars

It was long ago that Odin, Hoenir and Loki set out to go through the world together. Once when they were walking along the sea shore, they saw two tree trunks washed up on the beach in front of them. One of them was an ash tree and the other was an elm.

The three gods each gave a gift to the trees: Loki gave them blood and the look of life; Hoenir gave them a share of cleverness and wits; but Odin bent over each of them, and he breathed life into them.

Then the two first people, Ash the man and Elm the woman, stepped out into the world.

After this, All Father would look down over Midgarth from his high seat Lid Shelf, as his people went about their lives. Soon there were many of them across all the earth. They set up farms, they went hunting in the woods, and they were living happy peaceful lives.

Then Odin saw a stranger among the people.

Her name was Goldbright and wherever she went, people wanted gold. They craved gold. They hid it in secret places. They began to bicker about gold, to fight over gold, and even to kill each other for the sake of gold.

Odin grew angry.

He sent Loki to fetch Goldbright to his hall in Asgarth, and when she came into the hall, all the gods hurled spears at her. The spears went right through her, but she walked on unharmed towards the gods.

Then they pushed her into the fire, and Goldbright burnt down to nothing. But she stepped out of the fire again, alive and well.

Again they pushed her in, again she burnt down to nothing, and again she stepped out unharmed.

A third time too, it happened as before.

They let Goldbright go, because there was nothing they could do against her.

But Goldbright had come from the gods of the Vanir. Odin and his children are powerful gods, and are known as the Aesir. But it is the gods of the Vanir who rule over all the yearnings and cravings of people's hearts. When the Vanir knew what the Aesir had done to Goldbright, they got ready for war.

That was the first war that ever there was, when the Vanir pitted their spells and cunning against the strength of the Aesir. Odin threw his spear above the Vanir host, but they broke through the walls of Asgarth and trampled over the fields of the gods.

Then the Aesir asked for peace.

All of the gods, both Vanir and Aesir, gathered at the Seats of Judgement on Ida Field, and agreed to live in peace. And to be sure that this peace would last, they agreed that some of the Vanir should come to live among the Aesir as a pledge of peace, and some of the Aesir should live with the Vanir.

There was a big barrel there, and each of the gods went up in turn and spat in it, so that their spittle was mingled together in one barrel, just as they themselves were now mingled together as one people.

Odin chanted spells over the barrel until a man stepped out. This man was called Kvasir.

Because Kvasir was made from the spittle of all the gods, so he had the wisdom of all the gods. He set out through the world, bringing wisdom wherever he went.

Then the Vanir left.

Niord, the richest of the Vanir, stayed behind in Asgarth with the Aesir, and his two children, Frey and Freya, stayed there too. But the gods Hoenir and Mimir went away with the Vanir as a pledge of peace, and lived by their laws.

Hoenir was a fine-looking god; he stood tall, he walked proudly and he had a handsome face. He looked like a great chieftain, but he wasn't very clever. Every time the Vanir held a meeting, Mimir had to whisper in Hoenir's ear so that Hoenir would know what to say.

Mimir gave him good advice, and Hoenir repeated it at the meetings. But the Vanir noticed that Hoenir wouldn't say anything unless Mimir was with him, or he would just say 'Let everyone else decide.'

The Vanir killed Mimir and cut his head off, so that all Hoenir could say was, 'Let everyone else decide.' They sent him back, carrying Mimir's head in a bag.

When Hoenir came back to Asgarth, Odin took care of Mimir's head. He covered it in herbs and wrapped it in fine linen, and he put it in a pot. And because of the magic that Odin worked over that head, it can speak. Odin keeps it and questions it, and Mimir's head answers him with all the wisdom it ever had before.

So Mimir's wisdom is alive with the gods to this day.

Niord's Children

When the Aesir and Vanir made peace, the Vanir gave the god Niord as a pledge of goodwill, and with him came his two children Frey and Freya. Niord lives at Boat Town, and his children grew up there.

Niord's daughter is Freya, and she is very skilled in magic. She is the loveliest of goddesses, and she is known as the Lady of the Vanir.

Her home is in Folk Field where she has a hall called Seat Roomy; its benches are filled with her handmaidens and with warriors who have fallen in battle. She has a beautiful bower there too, where she sleeps. When her door is shut, no one can get in unless she lets them.

Freya is married to the god Oth, but Oth wanders over the earth and Freya weeps for his return. She walks through the world searching for him and when she weeps, her tears fall to the ground as pure gold. Freya and Oth have two daughters, and their names are Jewel and Treasure.

Freya has a wagon drawn by two cats, and she has a magic hawk skin. Whenever she puts on the hawk skin she takes the shape of a hawk, and she can fly wherever she wants across all worlds.

She also has a wonderful necklace called the Brising Necklace, which is finer and more beautiful than any other jewellery. This necklace was made by four dwarfs called Dvalin, Alfrik, Berling and Grer.

Freya first saw it when she was walking past a big stone. The door into the stone was open, and she saw the four dwarfs inside making the golden necklace. It was almost ready. Freya gazed at the necklace, and it was the most beautiful thing she had ever seen.

As soon as she saw the Brising Necklace, Freya wanted it for herself, so she asked the dwarfs if they would give it to her, but they would not. Then Freya said she would buy it, and she offered to give them vast stores of silver and gold. But the dwarfs only smiled and said, 'We do not need your gold. We have plenty to make trinkets like this one.'

Freya gazed at the necklace and she said, 'What do I have to do, to get it?'

The dwarfs gazed at Freya, and they said that they would take no payment for it unless she would spend a night with each of them, and they would not part with it for any other price.

The dwarfs were ugly, but the necklace was beautiful. The more Freya looked at the necklace, the more she felt it had to be hers. So she did as they asked, and that is how she won the Brising Necklace from the dwarfs.

But that necklace was stolen by Loki.

He saw that Freya had a splendid new necklace, and he could see how much she loved it. So he crept up to Freya's bower in the dead of night. Loki went all round the bower, and he could see no way in. But Loki can turn himself into whatever shape he wants, so he turned himself into a fly and then he found a way in through a tiny gap under the roof.

Inside, the goddess lay sleeping on her bed, and Loki landed on the pillow beside her. She was wearing the beautiful Brising Necklace, but the clasp was fastened behind her neck. Still in his fly shape, Loki stung her on the cheek, and she turned over in her sleep. Then he undid her necklace, opened up her bower doors and walked out.

Loki took the necklace, and ran off to the sea. He turned himself into a seal, and he swam until he came to the Singing Stone. He hid there with the necklace, beneath the waves by the Singing Stone.

Next morning, Freya woke to find her doors wide open and her necklace gone. But Heimdal, the Watchman of the Gods, who stands on Bifrost Bridge, looked out over

the world and he saw where Loki had gone in the shape
of a seal, and where he had hidden by the Singing Stone.

When Freya found her necklace was gone, Heimdal
turned himself into another seal and swam after Loki. The
two seals fought there, and they struggled with each other
until Heimdal took the golden Brising Necklace.

He brought it back and gave it to Freya again.

Freya's brother is Frey. He had also come to live in Asgarth with his father Niord. The gods gave him Elfhome as a teething gift. That is where he has his hall, and he is known as the Lord of Elves.

One day, Frey sat on All Father's high seat of Lid Shelf, and from there he could see across all the upper worlds. To the north in Etinhome he saw a beautiful building, and a lovely girl was going from the house out to her bower. When she raised her arms to let herself in, a light shone from her arms that spread over sea and sky, and brightened all the worlds.

Frey thought she was the most beautiful girl he had ever set eyes on. Straightaway, he fell deeply in love with her.

When he stepped down from Lid Shelf, Frey was sad and sick at heart because he had lost sight of the girl. And when he got home he wouldn't speak. He didn't sleep and he didn't eat, and nobody dared talk to him. He looked troubled. He scarcely seemed to know where he was. He hardly heard when people spoke to him.

Frey could do nothing but think about the girl he'd seen in Etinhome. Her name was Gerd, and she was the daughter of the etin Gymir and his wife Aurboda.

Niord didn't know what was wrong with his son. He asked Frey's servant Skirnir to help.

'You know him better than anyone,' he said, 'because you grew up side-by-side in one house together. If he'll tell anyone, it will be you. Find out who has made him so angry that he won't talk to anybody.'

'I don't think Frey will thank me for asking, but I'll do it for your sake,' said Skirnir.

So he went to Frey and said, 'What's troubling you, Frey? Why do you sit all alone by yourself? And why won't you talk to anyone?'

Frey said, 'Why should I tell you? How could you understand that the sunshine can light up the day, but not my heart?'

Skirnir said, 'It can't be so bad, if you won't tell me when we grew up side-by-side in one house together.'

Then Frey told Skirnir what he had done and that he had seen Gerd, and he said he could never be happy until he had made her his wife.

'Now you must go and ask her to marry me,' he said, 'and you must bring her back with you, whether her father agrees or not. And I'll pay you well for this.'

'Then give me your horse that will go through fire,' said Skirnir, 'and also your sword that will fight by itself.'

Frey said, 'I will give you anything, if you will help me win her as my wife. And you must do whatever you have to, so that she will marry me.'

Then Skirnir took Frey's sword and his horse Bloody Hoof, and away he rode to Etinhome. As he drew near to Gymir's farm, great flames flared up around the yard. There was a strong fence around it too, and the gates were guarded by snarling dogs. A shepherd was sitting on a mound nearby, and Skirnir said to him, 'How do I get past Gymir's dogs to see his daughter Gerd?'

The shepherd said, 'No one gets past those dogs to see Gerd. Turn back while you can! You will never speak with Gymir's wonderful daughter.'

But Skirnir rode on towards the farm. He rode through the flames on Bloody Hoof, and leapt over the fence. Then he got off his horse, and let it graze in the yard.

Gerd heard the noise in the yard, and she asked her maid to bring Skirnir inside. 'Are you a god or an elf?' she asked him, 'and why have you ridden through fire to meet me?'

Skirnir said, 'I have come from the gods, to bring you back as a bride for Frey.'

Gerd said, 'I will not go to meet the gods or marry Frey at any man's bidding. My life is here, and here I will stay.'

'I have brought you Apples of Life from Mimir's Wood. They will be yours if you will marry Frey.'

'I will not take an apple for any man's sake.'

'I'll give you a ring of gold that Odin has owned.'

'I won't have the ring which Odin owned. I do not think I am short of gold.'

Skirnir said, 'Do you see this shining sword? I'll cut off your head unless you come!'

Gerd said, 'You can do as you want, but I won't come with you.'

Then Skirnir took out a knife and a piece of wood, and he started to write in runes on the wood.

'I have been to the living wood, and brought back the branch of power. Now I carve these runes and this curse against you. Your wealth will wither and you will never be married. You will always want a man, and you will yearn for children. You'll sit out on the hillside wishing for death, howling with grief. Everything will stare at you. Odin will be angry with you, Frey will hate you. All this will be, if you will not marry him. I have carved this curse in runes, but I can undo it.'

Then Gerd gave Skirnir a drink of mead and she said, 'I never thought that I would love the Vanir. You may tell Frey that I will meet him nine nights from now in a grove on the island called Barrey, and there we will be married.'

So that was the news that Skirnir took back to tell Frey. And when he brought him this news, Frey was standing outside his door waiting for him.

Then Frey said, 'Three nights are long, six nights are longer, how can I last for nine?' But nine nights later he went to the island of Barrey, and he found his happiness there with Gerd.

The Apples of Life

Once when Odin, Hoenir and Loki were going through the world, they walked all day over bleak mountainsides and barren wastes in Etinhome, and it was hard for them to find anything to eat.

Early that evening, they came into a deep valley filled with lush grass and leafy oak trees, and grazing amongst the trees there was a great herd of oxen.

They thought it was a good find. So they chose a big fine-looking bull for themselves, and they slaughtered it for their supper. They dug a pit in the ground to make an earth oven, and gathered fallen branches for the fire. When it was hot enough, they rolled the body of the bull on top and covered it over with earth to cook.

Then when they thought it should be ready, they uncovered it to eat it. But the ox was not cooked at all. It was still just as raw as when they had put it in.

They covered the meat and waited again. They left it just as long as before, until they thought it would surely be done. But when they opened up their oven again, the ox was still uncooked. And when they tried to cut it open, they couldn't cut into it at all.

Odin said, 'What can be stopping this bull from cooking, and why can't we cut it up?'

Then they heard a voice in the oak tree above them, saying, 'It is I who am stopping the bull from cooking.'

They looked up. There was an eagle above them sitting in the branches of the tree, and it wasn't a little one.

'I am the etin Thiassi, and that ox is from my herd,' it said. 'You have killed one of my oxen, and it won't cook and you won't cut it, until you let me eat my full share.'

Odin asked Hoenir to cut the meat into four quarters, so each of them would have an equal share. But the eagle said, 'No, that bull is mine and I will take my own share for myself.' It dropped down from the tree, spread its wings over the bull and started to eat.

The eagle quickly ate up one shoulder, and it started on the next. It finished that shoulder too, and started on the legs. Then it got up onto the bull's rump to eat there.

Loki was watching this.

He thought the eagle was going to eat all the meat and leave nothing for the gods. He grabbed a stick and ran at the bird, and he whacked the eagle hard on the back.

The eagle pulled away, and flew up into the air. But the stick stuck fast to the eagle's back, and Loki found his hands were stuck to the stick, so the eagle flew off with Loki dangling beneath him.

The eagle swooped low over the mountainside so that Loki's legs and feet were dashed against the rocks, and his skin was torn on the thorns. He felt that his arms were being wrenched out of their sockets, and he was soon howling with pain. Loki cried out, 'Please, please stop! Let me down! I'll do anything you want.'

The eagle answered, 'I will not let you down, and you will never be free, unless you give me your solemn vow that you will bring me my sister Idun from Asgarth with her casket of Apples.'

'But Idun is married to Bragi,' said Loki. 'She belongs with the gods now, and her Apples keep us from ever growing old.'

The eagle swooped low again over the mountain so that Loki's feet smashed hard against the rocks. He gave a shriek of pain and then he said, 'Meet me in nine days in Mirkwood by Midgarth's walls, and I will have Idun and her Apples with me.'

Then the eagle let him go. His hand wasn't stuck to the stick anymore, and the stick wasn't stuck to the eagle's back, and Loki fell in a heap on the mountainside. He got himself up, and went back down to join the gods. They sat and ate together, but Loki said nothing about his promise to Thiassi.

Nine days later, Loki met Idun in Asgarth and said, 'Everyone says your Apples are best, but I know a tree near Midgarth's walls which grows apples that you will think well worth having. Come with me and see!'

Idun laughed. She plucks her Apples from the branches of Mimir's Wood, and they are proof against all the poisons that flow through that tree.

'My Apples are not just sweet to eat,' she said. 'Whoever tastes them will not grow old, but will stay forever young and strong.'

'Bring your own Apples with you then,' said Loki, 'so you can see which ones are best.'

Idun went with Loki out of Asgarth, and she took her Apples with her. They walked together across the Rainbow Bridge into Midgarth, where Loki led her into Mirkwood. And while they were still looking for the apple tree, the eagle Thiassi swooped from the sky, caught Idun up in his talons and carried her off.

It wasn't long before the gods noticed Idun was gone. Without her Apples, they soon began to look old, grey and haggard. But it was Bragi who missed her most of all. He called the gods to the Seats of Judgement to see what could be done to find his wife. They asked each other who had last seen Idun, and what might have happened to her.

Heimdal said, 'I saw Idun going across Bifrost Bridge into Midgarth. She had her Apples with her, and Loki was by her side. If anyone knows what has happened to Idun, I think it will be Loki.'

They caught Loki and dragged him before the gods. They said, 'Loki, you have brought old age and death on us by stealing Idun and her Apples. Now you must suffer death at our hands.'

Loki answered, 'But I didn't steal Idun away. She walked with me freely into Midgarth. When we got there, a huge eagle swooped out of the sky and carried her off. So it is the eagle who stole her, and it is the eagle who must be killed.'

Then the gods said, 'Loki, you led Idun away from us, and now you must find her and bring her back, or else you will suffer the full punishment yourself.'

Loki said, 'I will search through Etinhome until I find her, if Freya will lend me her hawk skin.'

The gods fetched Freya's hawk skin, and Loki put it on. He flew north until he came to Etinhome, and he went straight to the home of the etin Thiassi.

Thiassi lived at the top of a mountain called Blast Home. He went fishing every day, so Idun was left in Blast Home alone. Loki flew up to the mountaintop and he said, 'Idun, get ready. I have come to take you home to the gods.'

Idun looked at him coldly and said, 'I trusted you once, Loki. How can I trust you again?'

'What would you rather do?' asked Loki. 'Are you so happy in Blast Home that you want to stay here instead with Thiassi?'

So Idun agreed to go with Loki. He turned her into a nut. Then he grabbed the nut in his talons, and flew off as fast as he could towards Asgarth. But when Thiassi got home and found that Idun was gone, he set off after them.

Soon, Loki felt a great tempest blowing up behind him. He looked round and saw the eagle Thiassi coming after him, and the beat of his wings was like the breath of a storm.

When the gods saw the little hawk flying back with the nut, and the great eagle flying after it, they fetched brushwood and wood shavings and set them all around the wall of Asgarth.

As soon as the hawk was safely over the wall, it dropped to the ground. Then the gods set light to the wood shavings, and the flames flared up to the skies.

The eagle couldn't stop and, as it flew through the flames, its flight feathers were burnt and it crashed to the ground. Then the gods all gathered around, and killed the etin Thiassi there.

It was Bragi the Peacemaker who dealt the death blow, because the eagle had wronged him more than anyone by taking Idun his wife.

That was a very famous deed.

Idun was back in Asgarth. The gods, who had begun to look so old, now grew young and strong again. It seemed that Loki had managed to put right the wrongs he had done. But in Etinhome, Thiassi had a daughter.

Her name was Skadi, and when she heard what had happened to her father, she set out from Blast Home to meet the gods. Skadi came on her skis, and she had a shield and spear with her, and a helmet on her head.

She stood below the walls of Asgarth and she called out, 'You killed Thiassi, who had done no harm to any one of you. When you came to his land you stole his cattle, but Thiassi shared his meat with you. When he came to your land, you killed him cruelly when he could not defend himself. If you had fought him in a fair fight, there is not one amongst you who could have overcome him.

'I am Skadi, Thiassi's daughter, and now I ask for one of the gods to come out and fight me fairly. And when I have killed just one of you, then I will take that as payment for my father's death.'

Odin said, 'Skadi, Thiassi's daughter, another death cannot repay you for your loss. We will offer you payment for your father's life, and you may name your own price.'

Skadi said, 'You have taken my only friend from me, and no riches in gold or silver can ever make up for that. I do not want the payment you offer.'

66

Odin said, 'You have lost the father who brought joy to your life, and we cannot bring him back to you. But you have no husband. You may choose any one of us to be your man, and if you find a husband to your liking, then maybe you will think you have been better paid by his life than you could have been by his death.'

Skadi said, 'Even if I found a husband I liked, it would never change the grief I feel in my heart. I will never know laughter or happiness again, since you have killed my father. I do not want the payment you offer.'

Odin said, 'Skadi, if you will take a husband among us, and if you will join us at our table and in our games, perhaps you will laugh with us and then you will be fully paid.'

Skadi said, 'Now you have offered what you cannot give. You can never pay me with my own laughter, and I will not laugh again. But you have a son called Balder, who is the gentlest and most beautiful of gods. So I will choose myself a husband, and if I laugh just once when I am with you then we will live together, but if not then he must die.'

So Skadi came in through the gates of Asgarth to choose her husband. But the gods put a heavy veil over her eyes so that she could only see the ground, and they all stood barefoot in front of her. Skadi looked down at their feet and she had to choose her husband without seeing any more than that.

Then she saw a very beautiful pair of feet, and she reached out saying, 'I choose you. There can't be much that's ugly about Balder!'

But it wasn't Balder. It was Niord who lives at Boat Town, where his feet are washed by the waters of the sea, and his were the most beautiful feet among the gods.

Skadi and Niord were married, and the gods held a great feast for their wedding. There was plenty to eat and drink, and plenty of fun and games.

They asked Skadi to join in the wedding games. No one was better at skiing or at shooting with a bow than she was, but still no one could make her laugh, and everyone was worried about what would happen to Niord.

Then Loki tied himself to a goat and pretended to wrestle with it, and all the gods laughed as they pulled this way and that, with the goat heaving one way and Loki tugging the other. The goat was bleating and Loki was howling and the gods were laughing, until Loki fell head first into Skadi's lap and she too burst out laughing.

Then the payment had been paid in full for Thiassi's death, but Odin also did this for Skadi: He took Thiassi's eyes, and he threw them up into the sky and made two stars out of them, which shine down on us to this day.

After Skadi and Niord were married, they agreed that they should live nine nights in the mountains at Blast Home, and the next nine nights by the sea at Boat Town.

But when Niord came back from Blast Home he said, 'I hate it in the mountains! It was only nine nights, but the howling of wolves seemed so ugly to me, when I thought of the song of the swans.'

But Skadi said, 'I could never sleep by the shoreside, because of the seabirds' shrieking. Every morning that gull flies in from the sea, and wakes me in my bed.'

So Skadi went back to the mountains alone, and she lives at Blast Home by herself.

Loki's Children

When Loki had first come to Asgarth, the gods said he should choose a wife and live among them, and Loki agreed to that. He married Sigyn, and they had two sons together whose names were Nari and Vali.

But Loki already had a wife in Etinhome. Her name was Ill Boding, and Loki had three children with her.

When Odin found out that Loki had children in Etinhome, he spoke with Mimir's head and he learned that they would bring evil to the gods. So, All Father sent the gods to fetch these children and bring them to him.

Then the gods went into Etinhome. They caught Loki's children there, and they brought them back to Odin.

The three children were a snake, a woman and a wolf.

That snake is the Great Monster. Odin took it and threw it into the deepest ocean. There it grew beneath the sea, until it became so big that it wrapped itself right around the Earth, and it grips its tail in its teeth just as a buckle would grip a belt. So it is known as the Midgarth Serpent and the World's Belt.

The second of Loki's children was a girl. Her name is Hel, and she is Death. Her face is deathly pale and blotched with black and bluish grey; she looks rather grim. Death has no place in Asgarth, where the gods live for ever, so Odin threw her into Shadow Home, and he set her to rule over the realms of Death. Hel has a hall there on Corpse Sands which is called Sleet Fall. Her doorstep is called Stumbling Block, and her bed is called Sick Bed. She has a plate called Hunger, and a knife called Famine.

The third child was a wolf cub called Fenrir. The gods didn't have the heart to throw it out, so they took it in and kept it. Tyr looked after the cub and fed it every day.

The cub grew and thrived, and soon it was bigger than most wolves. Then only Tyr dared go near it, because the wolf cub was snappy and its teeth were sharp.

When the gods saw how big the wolf was growing, they remembered that Mimir had foretold that it would do them harm, so they settled on a plan. They made a leash to bind the wolf, a thick iron chain. It was very strong and heavy, and they called it Leyding.

They took it to the wolf and said, 'Fenrir, you are bigger and stronger than other wolves. Let's play a game to test your strength. This leash is called Leyding. We'll put it on you, and you try to break it.'

The wolf looked at the leash. It was rather big, but he thought he was strong enough to break it, so he let them do what they wanted. They fastened the leash around Fenrir's foot and sank the other end in the earth.

The wolf tugged against the leash. It sprang apart at his first kick, and Fenrir laughed.

'I've got loose from Leyding!' he said.

Then the gods made a leash that was twice as strong, and they called it Dromi. They dragged that to the wolf and said, 'You broke the first leash, so we thought you'd like to play the game again. This leash is called Dromi. Your strength will be famous, if you can break such sturdy handiwork as this.'

The wolf looked at the leash. It seemed much stronger than the last one. But he had grown since then, and he thought he'd never be famous if he didn't take any risks. So he let them put that leash on him too.

They fastened Dromi around Fenrir's foot, and sank the other end in the earth. When the gods said they were ready, the wolf shook himself and dashed the leash against the ground. He yanked at it and jerked hard against it. He kicked with his feet, and it flew into pieces that scattered far and wide.

Then the wolf laughed. 'I have done for Dromi!' he said.

After that the gods were worried that they would never be able to bind Fenrir. They had made the strongest leash they could, and the wolf had broken it.

Then All Father sent Frey's messenger Skirnir down to the dwarfs to get them to make a new leash. This leash was not made of iron nor any other metal. It was made from cat's footsteps and from woman's beard, from mountain roots and bear sinews, from fish's breath and bird's spittle. And to this day, you'll be hard put to see or hear any one of those things.

The new leash was called Gleipnir, and it was as thin and smooth as a silken string. When Skirnir brought it back to the gods, they thanked him heartily for it. Then the gods took the wolf out onto an island called Heath in the lake that is called Utter Darkness.

There they showed him the silky string and they said, 'First you broke Leyding, and now you have broken Dromi. This leash is called Gleipnir, and we'd like you to try your strength with it.'

'You brought me a big leash and I broke it,' said Fenrir. 'Then you brought me a bigger leash and I broke that too. But this is just a little ribbon, and I can't see how I'll be famous for breaking that! So, no. I don't want you to put it on me.'

'It's tougher than it looks,' they said, and they passed it round and tugged at it to show that it didn't break, 'but you'll be able to break it.'

The wolf said, 'I could see the strength in Leyding and Dromi, but Gleipnir is just a grey ribbon. If there is strength in it, it must be made with cunning and trickery. So although it looks thin, I want nothing to do with it. It's not going on my foot!'

The gods said, 'Surely, when you have broken such great iron chains, you're not scared of a little ribbon like this? And if you can't even snap this string, then we'll have nothing to fear from you, so we'll let you go again.'

The wolf said, 'If you bind me so that I can't get free, then I reckon you'll sneak off and leave me here. But I don't want you to say that I'm scared, so if one of you will put his right hand in my mouth as a mark of trust, then you can put the leash on me.'

The gods all looked at each other and none of them wanted to offer his hand, until Tyr stretched out his right hand and put it between the wolf's open jaws. Then they fastened the leash Gleipnir around Fenrir's foot.

The wolf shook himself and kicked at it but, as he pulled, the leash tightened. He yanked and he strained at Gleipnir but, the more he struggled the tighter it grew, and there was nothing he could do to break it.

Then the gods all laughed and they said, 'Gleipnir has got you!'

But Tyr didn't laugh, because he had lost his hand.

When they knew the wolf was really stuck, the gods took a loop called Noose from the leash Gleipnir, and they drew it through a great slab of rock called Yell, and sank it deep in the earth. Then they got a big stone called Thviti and used it to peg the rock even deeper under the earth. The wolf stretched wide his jaws and strained to bite at them, but the gods shoved a sword in his mouth with the tip pointing upwards, so he cannot close his mouth.

He is there still, howling horribly, and the slaver running from his jaws makes the river called Hope which flows through all worlds. And there he will stay until the Doom of the Powers.

Loki's Wager

Thor's wife is called Sif. She is the most beautiful of goddesses, and her hair is like gold. So Loki did this out of sheer naughtiness: He cut off Sif's hair.

He broke into her bower by turning himself into a fly, just as once he had broken into Freya's bower to steal the Brising Necklace, and he cut off all Sif's hair while she was sleeping. So when she woke up, she was bald.

When Thor caught up with Loki after that, he picked him up in his hands, and his brows sank low over his eyes.

'You cut off Sif's hair,' he said. 'Now, I'm going to break every bone in your body!'

Loki was terrified.

'I'll get her new hair,' he said. 'I'll go to the dwarfs and they'll make new hair, and it will look just as nice, I promise.'

So Thor let him go.

Loki ran off, and his shoes took him over sea and sky until he reached a cave. He went down through that cave into the depths of Black Elfhome, which lies under Asgarth.

There is a deep cavern there, where the sons of Ivaldi live. Their cave is lit with blazing fire, and the walls ring with the sound of their hammers and the wheezing of their bellows that breathe life and heat into the fires of their forge.

'Sons of Ivaldi,' said Loki, 'your fame has spread through the Nine Worlds as far as Asgarth. You boast that you can make whatever you want, and that there is nothing anyone could ask for, which you cannot make. I come as a messenger from the gods to see if this is true.'

'It is true,' said the sons of Ivaldi.

'Then you must prove it,' said Loki. 'You must make what seems unmakeable. Make me a head of hair out of pure beaten gold that is just as fine as the best of hair, so that if you put it onto a bald head it will take root and start to grow just like real hair.'

The sons of Ivaldi set to work making golden hair for Sif. When they had finished, Loki thought how easy it had been to get the dwarfs to make the hair, so he told them to make a wonderful ship and a spear for the gods as well.

And the dwarfs made them just to prove they could.

When the sons of Ivaldi had made these things, Loki said, 'Now I shall take these wonders back to the gods in Asgarth, so they can see for themselves that the tales we have heard are true.' And off he went.

On his way through Black Elfhome, Loki met a dwarf called Brokk.

'What has brought you here, Loki?' asked the dwarf. 'And where are you taking these treasures?'

'I am sent from the gods,' said Loki. 'I am carrying gifts to Asgarth, that were made by the sons of Ivaldi. And they're better than anything that you and your brother Sindri could make.'

'Indeed, they are not!' said Brokk. 'My brother is the best of smiths.'

'I'll wager my head that he cannot make three gifts for the gods as fine as these,' said Loki.

'And I wager my head that he can,' said Brokk.

'Then the gods shall judge whose gift is best,' said Loki.

So that was their wager.

Each of them had bet his head that he would be the one to bring the finest gift to the gods. The gods were to be the judges, and whoever lost the bet would lose his head.

Brokk went off to Sindri's workshop, and he told his brother what he'd done.

'You'd better start blowing at the bellows then,' said Sindri.

Brokk set to work, and the fire of Sindri's forge blazed in the breeze from his bellows.

When Sindri thought the fire was hot enough, he took the skin of a pig and put it in the forge. Then he said, 'I'm going out now, but you have to stay and keep those bellows blowing until I take my work out again, or it will be spoiled. And if you fail, it will be your head that pays for it.'

As soon as the smith left, a little fly buzzed in and it landed on Brokk's wrist and started to bite. Brokk didn't stop to brush it off, but went on blowing at the bellows with the fly biting hard at his wrist.

When the smith came back, he took his work out of the forge. It was a living pig, a boar with bristles of shining gold.

Then the smith put gold into the fire.

He said to Brokk, 'You keep blowing, and don't stop till I get back!' And he went out again.

Brokk was still working at the bellows. It was hard work and it was hot work beside the burning forge. The fly came in again, and this time it landed on the back of his neck. And if it bit him hard before, it bit twice as hard now. But still Brokk kept up his work at the bellows.

When the smith came in again, he took a gold arm ring from the forge, a heavy ring of solid gold.

Then Sindri took iron, and he put that in the fire.

'You keep blowing at the bellows while I go out,' he said, 'and if you stop for even a moment, then the work will be spoiled.'

In came the fly, and now it landed in the corner of Brokk's eye. It bit on his eyelid until the blood ran. And when the blood trickled into his eye so he could hardly see, Brokk swiped at it quickly with his hand.

The fly flew off, and Brokk went straight back to work.

This time when the smith came back, he went to the forge and he took a hammer out of the fire. He looked at it for some time. Then he said, 'It's a little too short in the handle, and I think you must have stopped in your work for a while, but perhaps it will still be good enough.'

Sindri gave those three fine things to Brokk.

'Now go, brother!' he said. 'Take these gifts to the gods and win your bet.'

And Brokk took them straight to Asgarth, to show them to the gods.

The gods took their places at the Seats of Judgement on Ida Field, for Brokk and Loki to show them their fine gifts. Thor, Odin and Frey were the judges, and whoever they chose was to be the winner.

First Loki brought out the golden hair, and it took root as soon as it touched the skin of Sif's head. And even Thor agreed that this was a wonder.

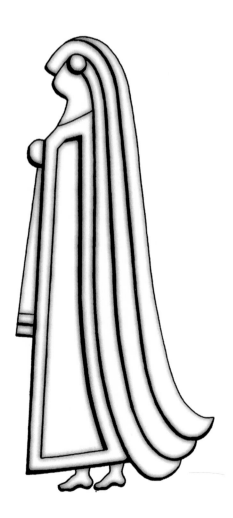

Then Loki brought out the spear and he gave that to Odin. He said, 'Odin, the name of this spear is Flincher. It will never stop in its thrust, no matter how hard the thing you thrust against.'

Then he gave the ship to Frey. He said, 'Frey, the name of this ship is Ski Blader, and it will always have a fair breeze to fill the sail and take you wherever you want to go. It will be big enough for you and all the gods to go aboard with your weapons and war-gear, but if you want you can fold it up like a napkin and put it in your pocket.'

Then Brokk brought out his gifts.

He gave the arm ring to Odin and he said, 'Odin, this ring is called Dripper. Every ninth night it will drip another eight gold rings just as heavy as it is itself.'

To Frey he gave the pig. He said, 'This boar is called Golden Bristle. He's faster than any horse, and he'll run over sea and sky by day or by night, because it's never so dark that the glow of his bristles won't light your way.'

Then he went up to Thor and he gave him the hammer. He said, 'Thor, the hammer is called Miller. You can hit as hard as you like with it, and it won't break. Whatever you throw it at, it will never miss. And no matter how far it goes, it will always come straight back to your hand again. But if you want, it can be so small that you can wear it under your shirt. There's only one thing wrong with it,' he added. 'The handle is a bit short.'

Then all the gifts had been given, and the gods spoke among themselves about which was best. Odin was pleased with both his gifts, and so was Frey. Thor was very happy to see Sif with her hair again, but he couldn't wait to try out his new hammer.

The gods said, 'We like all the gifts very much, and we thank you both for all of them. But if we have to choose just one then we choose the hammer, because with that hammer, Thor can keep us safe from frost etins. So, the dwarf wins.'

Brokk smiled. He took his axe and stepped up to Loki.

Loki said, 'Wouldn't it be better, Brokk, if I gave you gold? I think my head looks best where it is. What use could it be to you?'

'No chance!' said Brokk.

'Catch me, then!' said Loki.

Loki had his shoes on, and he ran off into the air so that when Brokk tried to catch him, he was far out of reach. Then the dwarf asked Thor to fetch him back. So Storm Rider got into his wagon, and his two goats Tooth Gnasher and Tooth Grinder drew him into the skies after Loki.

When Thor brought him back, Brokk raised his axe above Loki's head. But Loki said, 'Wait! It's true that I did bet my head, so that belongs to you. But I didn't say anything about my neck. My neck is still my own, and I don't want it damaged in any way whatsoever.'

Brokk couldn't think of a way to cut Loki's head off without cutting through the neck. He said, 'My new head is full of lies and tricks. I'll stitch the lips together, so it can't speak.'

The dwarf took out a thong and a knife, and he tried to make holes in Loki's lips to sew them up, but the knife wouldn't cut. Then he said, 'Knife, I wish your brother Awl were here!'

As soon as he said that, the awl was there in his hand and then the dwarf made the holes in Loki's lips, and he used his thong to lace them together.

The thong that Brokk used is called Unyielding. It's very strong, and Loki could neither cut it nor break it. He had to tear through his lips to get it out, and they are still ragged even to this day.

Thor the Bride

Thor was angry when he woke up and couldn't find his hammer. His beard shook and his hair bristled as he groped around for it.

'Loki!' he yelled, 'It's gone! It's nowhere on earth and it's not in heaven. Someone has stolen my hammer!'

Loki could see the fire burning in Thor's eyes.

'I can help you, Thor,' he said. 'With Freya's feather cloak, I'll fly through the air like a hawk till I find it.'

They went off to Freya's beautiful bower, and Thor called out, 'Freya, you have to lend Loki your feather cloak, so he can fetch my hammer back!'

'Of course!' said Freya. 'I would lend it gladly, even if it were made of gold or silver.'

Loki put on the feather cloak, and he took the shape of a hawk. Then he flew and the feathers whirred, until he had left behind the land of the gods and he came to Etinhome.

Thrym, Lord of Etins, was sitting outside on a mound of earth, twisting gold into collars for his dogs, and trimming his horses' manes. He looked hard at the hawk. In all its feathers it was just like a hawk, but its eyes were the eyes of a man.

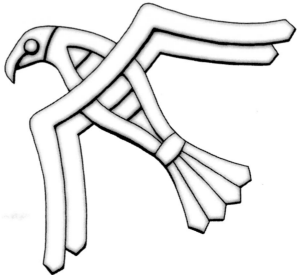

'Loki,' he called, 'how are the gods? How are the elves? And what brings you here to Etinhome?'

'It's not good with the gods. It's not good with the elves. Have you taken Storm Rider's hammer and hidden it somewhere?'

86

Thrym laughed. 'I have taken Storm Rider's hammer, and he won't see it again, because I've buried it eight miles deep beneath this mound. No one will ever get it back, unless they bring me Freya for my wife!'

'Is there nothing else the gods can give you to get the hammer back?' said Loki.

'No,' said Thrym. 'I've got golden-horned cattle; I've got the blackest of bulls; I've got plenty of treasures. The only thing I want is to have Freya as my wife.'

Loki flew and the feathers whirred, until he had left behind the land of the etins and he came back to Asgarth.

Thor met him before he landed and he called out, 'How did it go? Tell me the news while you're still on the wing, before you can sit down and spin me a tale.'

'Thrym, Lord of Etins, has got your hammer,' said Loki. 'He won't give it back unless he gets Freya as his bride.'

They went off to Freya's beautiful bower, and Thor called out, 'Freya, get ready! Put on your bridal clothes! Get dressed to greet the etin Thrym! You're coming to Etinhome to be married.'

Freya was angry when she heard that. She snorted with rage and her bower shook. The Brising Necklace burst from her neck.

'The gods would think I was mad,' she said, 'if I went off with you to marry an etin!'

Thor called the gods to their Seats of Judgement.

'You have to tell Freya to marry Thrym,' he said, 'or I'll never get my hammer back!'

'We can't send Freya to Etinhome,' said Odin, 'But Thor must have his hammer, to keep us safe from the etins.'

Heimdal said, 'We'll dress Thor up in bridal clothes, put the Brising Necklace around his neck, and drape a fine veil from his fierce brow. Then he can go in Freya's place.'

'But the gods will think I'm soft,' said Thor, 'if you dress me up in women's clothes.'

But Loki said, 'Shut up, Thor! The etins could be here any moment, if you don't have your hammer to save us all.'

So they wrapped Thor up in fine white linen, and put a pretty dress on him trimmed with silk. They put the Brising Necklace around his thick neck, and a beautiful brooch on his broad chest. They put a dainty bride's veil over his head, to hide his bushy red beard and his fierce red eyes.

Loki looked at Thor, and he begged, 'Can I be your bridesmaid? Then we'll both go together to Etinhome!'

So Loki got dressed up to go with him.

Thor fetched his two goats Tooth Gnasher and Tooth Grinder, and hitched them to his wagon. The goats pulled them up into the air, and Thor and Loki set off for Etinhome. The lightning flashed and thunder rang out around them through the skies.

Thrym looked up from his mound in Etinhome and he called out, 'Get up, etins! Get everything ready! Here comes Freya to be my bride!'

He watched Thor's wagon as it landed, and saw two fine ladies getting down. Thor strode out towards the hall with his dress flapping in the wind, and his bridesmaid tripped along prettily behind.

Soon it was evening, and they all went inside for the wedding feast. Etins had gathered there from all over Etinhome, and there was plenty to eat and plenty to drink, because etins are always hungry.

Thrym asked Freya to join the feast, and Thor didn't need to be asked twice. He ate a whole ox and eight salmon, before he remembered he should be eating from the ladies' table. Then he ate up half the snacks there too.

Everyone stopped to stare at Freya.

'Was there ever a bride who could eat like this?' asked Thrym.

The clever bridesmaid found a quick answer. 'Freya hasn't eaten for eight whole days, because she longed to come to Etinhome, so perhaps she's a little bit hungry.'

Then Thrym was happy. He watched his Freya turn to look for drink. She picked up a barrel and guzzled eight gallons of mead in one go.

'Was there ever a bride who could drink like this?' asked Thrym.

Loki said, 'Freya hasn't drunk a drop for eight whole days, because she was so keen to meet you, so she might be a little bit thirsty.'

Now everything was ready for the wedding but, before the ceremony, Thrym thought he'd like to kiss his bride. He stepped forward and lifted Freya's veil, but he jumped back when he saw Thor's fierce eyes staring out at him.

Thrym turned to the bridesmaid and asked, 'Was there ever a bride with eyes so fiery and red?'

Loki said, 'Freya hasn't slept a wink for eight whole nights, because she was so eager to marry you, so her eyes could be slightly red.'

'Let's get on with the wedding,' said Thrym. 'Fetch me my wedding ring!'

Thrym's etin sister scurried in with the ring for him to give to Freya. Then she turned to the bride, who was still sitting eating.

'Don't forget,' she said, 'you'll have to take off your ring too, to give it to Thrym!'

'Now, bring in the hammer to bless the bride!' said Thrym, 'Lay Miller in her lap, so that together we can bless these rings!'

Then the etins brought in the hammer, and laid it gently in the lap of the bride.

Storm Rider laughed in his heart when he saw his own hammer brought to him, and laid in his lap. He grabbed it in his hand, and threw off Freya's veil.

Thor hurled that hammer straight at Thrym. He killed Thrym first, the Lord of Etins, and then he felled the rest of the etins there.

Thor and Loki leapt back into the wagon, and they rode home over sea and sky to Asgarth with the hammer.

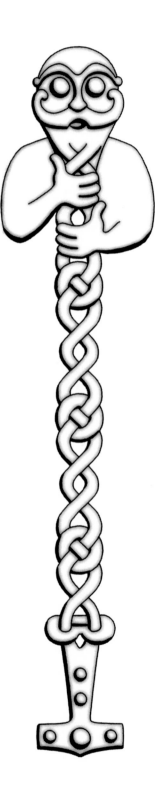

The Builder's Fee

It was the last day of summer. Thor had gone off with his hammer to thrash trolls in Etinhome, but the other gods were gathered at the Seats of Judgement in Bright Home.

A builder came to them then, who said he could build them a wall around Asgarth which would be so strong that they'd be safe and sound in their stronghold against attacks by rock etins and frost etins, even if they had already broken through the walls of Midgarth.

'I can build that wall for you before two winters are over,' he said, 'and in payment, I want to have the Sun and the Moon, and I want Freya for my wife.'

The gods didn't want to pay the fee that the builder had asked for, but they did want a wall against the etins. Yet it was hard to believe that anyone could build such a wall around all Asgarth in only two winters.

In the end Odin told the builder, 'If you can build the whole wall by yourself in just one single winter, then you will get the fee you have asked for. But you must work alone without anyone to help you, and if there is anything left unfinished on the first day of summer, then you will get nothing.'

The builder said, 'I'll take up your offer and I'll have no man to help me, but you must let me have the help of my horse.'

The Aesir were uneasy about this, but Loki said, 'Let him have his horse, or we'll never get our wall.'

Then they swore oaths to each other. The builder swore to make the wall in a single winter with only his horse to help him, and the gods swore to pay him with the Sun and the Moon and with Freya as his bride.

The builder also wanted the gods to swear they would keep him safe while he was working in Asgarth, even if Thor came back from Etinhome. Then All Father swore an oath on his holy ring, Dripper, that he would be safe and that they would pay him for his work.

So on the first day of winter the builder set to work, and he had the help of no man but only the help of his horse. The gods were amazed at the size of the stones that he heaved into place for that wall. But it wasn't what the builder did that shocked the gods, so much as what his horse could do.

The builder's horse was called Stumbler, and he did twice the work that the builder could do. Every evening, the builder drove his horse off to fetch stone for the wall, and the gods would watch in wonder at the huge rocks the horse dragged back.

Day after day, week after week, the work went on both by day and by night, and the wall around Asgarth grew tall and strong like a sheer cliff, until everyone could see that the builder's work would be finished on time.

No one could have made a stronger wall to keep the etins out. But surely only an etin could do such work! This builder and his horse had the strength of etins. Were they not both etins from Etinhome, that had come to cheat the gods of the Sun, the Moon and the goddess Freya?

When there were just three more days of winter left, the wall stretched almost all the way around Asgarth and the builder was ready to start work on the gateway.

Then the gods went again to their Seats of Judgement. They asked, 'Who was it who said that the Sun and Moon should be stripped from the Sky? And who said that Freya should be sent away to Etinhome? Whoever it was,' they said, 'he must pay for it with his life!'

Heimdal said, 'The one who had most to do with this was the one who is behind most wickedness in Asgarth, and that is Loki.'

The gods said that Loki should suffer an evil death for that, and Loki threw himself on his knees and begged for mercy.

Odin said, 'Loki, the judgement of the gods is against you, but if you can find some way to stop the builder from carrying off these treasures, then you may go free.'

'I'll find a way that you don't have to pay up,' said Loki, 'no matter what it might cost me.'

That evening, when the builder drove off for stone with his horse Stumbler, another horse darted out from the woods, ran right up to Stumbler and whinnied.

Stumbler saw that it was a mare. He caught her scent on the night air, and he was mad to be with her. He broke the ropes that held him, and he ran to her. But as he ran towards her, the mare ran off into the woods.

The builder ran after his horse, the horse ran after the mare, and the mare ran deeper into the woods. The more Stumbler chased after the mare, the further she led him away from the world of Asgarth, away from the builder and his wall. The three of them ran all night through the woods, but the builder was furthest behind.

No work was done on the wall that night, while the builder was looking for his horse. Next morning, he came back alone. The work went slowly then, and there was no new stone at the workplace that day.

When evening came, the builder looked at the gap that was left in the wall. It was only a little gap, but there was only a single day left to fill it.

He knew that without his horse, he could never finish his work on time. And as he looked at that gap in the wall, he grew angry. He had built nearly the whole wall, but now he would never get his fee. Then the etin mood came over him. He stood up on top of his wall, and started hurling down stones into Asgarth.

'I'll break down Asgarth's Wall!' he shouted. 'I'll smash all Asgarth! I'll knock down Bright Home!'

Then they knew for sure that this was an etin.

When the gods saw that, they overlooked their promise to keep him safe, and they called on Thor. He was still out in Etinhome killing trolls, but as soon as they spoke his name, he was there among them. And when Thor saw an etin raging at the gates of Asgarth, he raised his hammer and hurled it without a second thought.

That was how Thor paid the etin's fee; not with the Sun and Moon and Freya as his bride, but with a hammer blow, so that his skull was smashed to pieces and he was sent down to Shadow Home, the world of the dead.

No one saw Loki for some time after that.

Summer passed by and winter came on, and still Loki did not come home. But next summer, Loki came out of the woods, and behind him he was leading a little grey foal.

Loki can turn himself into whatever he wants, and he had turned himself into the mare that Stumbler had followed. So it was Loki who was the mother of the foal. But Loki's foal was unlike other horses. It had eight legs.

Loki led the horse in among the gods. He walked right up to where All Father was sitting, and gave the horse to Odin. That horse is called Slider, and Odin rides him through the skies and across the seas.

He is the best of horses among gods and men.

Thor's Trip to Outgarth

Loki told Thor that there was a king in Etinhome called Outgarth Loki, who said that the etins of Outgarth were stronger than Thor himself.

'That's something we'll have to see,' said Thor.

He set off straightaway with his goats and his wagon, and Loki went with him as his guide. They rode through the skies, and the thunder rang out around them.

That evening they came to a farmer's house, where they stayed for the night. The farmer was called Egil, and he lived there with his wife and two children, a boy called Thialfi and a girl called Roeskva.

It was a poor farm, and there wasn't much food to go round. So Thor took his two goats, Tooth Grinder and Tooth Gnasher, and slaughtered them both. He flayed the skins from the goats, and set the meat to boil in a pot on the fire. When it was done, Thor carefully spread the skins on the ground away from the fire.

Thor and his friend sat down to eat, and he asked the farmer and his family to join them for supper.

'Come and eat with me,' he said, 'and share my food. But take care of the bones, and lay them on the skins here.'

They all thanked Thor, and sat down to eat. The farmer and the farmer's wife, the two children and Loki ate one of the goats, and Thor had the other one. Loki saw that Thialfi had a thigh bone in his hands. He had eaten the meat, and now he was turning the bone over in his hands, thinking of the tasty marrow inside.

Loki leaned over and said, 'Thor won't let you eat that. Look how much he's keeping for himself. He's eating a whole goat, while we all have to make do with one between us.'

Then Thialfi got a good grip on the bone, split it open with his knife and scooped out the marrow. He put the bone down on the skin with the others.

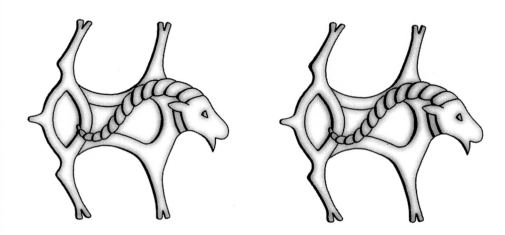

Thor slept there that night, and in the darkness before dawn he got up and dressed. He went over to where the bones were lying in heaps on the goatskins, away from the embers of the fire. Then he took out his hammer, and he raised it up over the bones to bless them.

The two goats sprang up alive and well, and Thor petted their heads and stroked their backs, but he found that one of them had a broken leg.

Thor frowned. 'One of you has broken your word to me,' he said, 'and broken the bone of one of my goats'

You can guess how scared the farmer was, when he saw Thor's brows sink down over his eyes. But when he saw the look in Thor's eyes, he thought he would drop down dead with sheer fright. Storm Rider's fist was clenched so tight round his hammer that his knuckles were white.

The farmer and his family cried out and begged for mercy. He fell to his knees and said, 'Please spare us! We'll give you anything you want.'

When Thor saw how scared they were, his anger left him and he calmed down. But as payment, he took their children from them, Thialfi and Roeskva. They became Thor's servants, and they have followed him ever since.

Thor was keen to get on with his trip to Outgarth, but he couldn't go in his wagon because his goat was lame. So he left his goats at Egil's farm and set off for Etinhome on foot.

He took Loki and Thialfi with him, and they walked all the way to the sea. Then he set out over the deepest ocean and, when he came to land he went ashore. They hadn't gone far when they reached a big wood, and they walked all day through the wood.

They made good going. Thialfi was the fastest of lads and he carried Thor's bag with their food in it. But they didn't know where they were going to stay that night.

They were still looking for somewhere to stay when it was getting dark. After a while, they found an empty house with a wide open doorway that stretched from one side to the other. They went inside and settled down to sleep, but in the middle of the night they were woken by a terrible rumbling. The ground beneath them was shaking, and the building shuddered with the noise.

Thor got up and looked around. He found that there were long thin rooms at the back of the house, and there was also a shorter side-room where Loki and Thialfi could lie down. Thor sat up in the doorway and kept watch, with his hammer ready in his hand. They heard terrible groanings and rumblings all night long.

When daylight came, Thor looked out and saw someone lying nearby in the woods, and he was not small. He was sound asleep and was snoring loudly. And every time this giant snored, the ground shook and the trees shuddered.

Then Thor knew what the noises had been in the night. He put on his belt of strength and took up his hammer, meaning to finish him right away, but just then the big etin woke up and sprang to his feet.

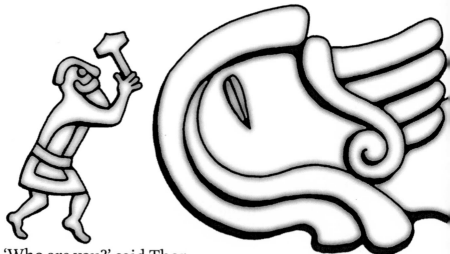

'Who are you?' said Thor.

'My name is Skrymir,' he said, 'but I don't need to ask your name; I can see you're the god Thor. Have you been in my glove?'

Skrymir reached out and picked up his glove, and then Thor saw that he had used it to stay the night in, and that the side-room where Loki and Thialfi had slept was the thumb of the glove.

Thor was just wondering how he could get rid of Skrymir when the etin asked, 'Shall I come with you and keep you company?'

'Yes,' said Thor.

Then Skrymir undid his knapsack and started to eat his breakfast. Thor and his friends went a little way off to have their own breakfast by themselves.

'Let's put all our food together in one bag,' said Skrymir.

'Yes,' said Thor.

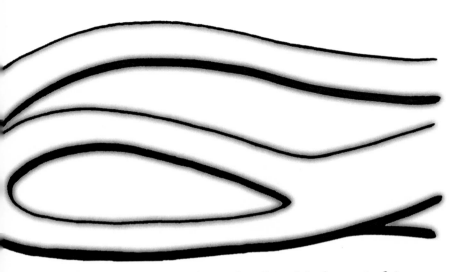

Skrymir put all their food in his bag, tied it up and slung it on his back. They walked all day, and the etin took great strides, so that Thor had to run to keep up.

In the evening he took them to a huge oak tree. 'We'll stop here and rest for the night,' he said, 'I'm ready for bed myself, but you take the bag and get yourselves some supper.'

Skrymir stretched himself out on the ground and fell fast asleep, and the branches of that oak tree were soon shaking with the sound of his snores.

Thor picked up the bag and started to untie the knot. But no matter how hard he tried, no matter which strap he tugged at, the knot just got tighter. When Thor saw he was getting nowhere, he got angry. He seized his hammer Miller in both hands, stepped up to Skrymir and knocked him on the head.

Skrymir opened one eye. 'Did a leaf just fall on me, Thor?' he asked. 'I guess you'll have eaten by now, and you'll be ready for your beds.'

'Yes,' said Thor. 'We're just on our way to bed now.'

Thor and his men went off to another oak and settled down to rest. But they couldn't sleep. In the middle of the night when Skrymir was snoring so loud that the whole forest rumbled, Thor got up and swung his hammer down hard on Skrymir's head. It was dark, but he felt it sink right into the etin's skull.

Just then, Skrymir looked up and said, 'What was that now? Did an acorn fall on me? And what are you doing, Thor? It's not time to be up already, is it?'

'No,' said Thor, stepping back quickly. 'I just woke up. It's the middle of the night. It's still time to sleep.' But he thought to himself that if he got another chance to hit that etin, Skrymir would never open his eyes again.

A little before dawn, he heard Skrymir snoring. Thor jumped up and swung his hammer with all his strength at Skrymir's head, so that it sank in right up to the handle.

Skrymir sat up and rubbed his head saying, 'There must be some birds awake up above me. I'm sure something fell on my head from the branches just now and woke me. Are you up already, Thor? It must be time to get going now, I suppose.'

'Yes,' said Thor.

'Don't worry. There's not far to go now before you get to Outgarth,' said Skrymir. 'But listen! If you do get to Outgarth, you'll see some big lads there. So don't act up, because Outgarth Loki's men won't put up with any nonsense from little lads like you. You can still turn back and go home. But if you're sure you want to go on, then you'll have to go east. My road goes north, through the mountains.'

Skrymir picked up the bag and slung it over his back. Then he set off into the wood. The gods didn't say they hoped to see him soon.

Thor and his men went on till about midday, when they saw the walls of Outgarth on the plain in front of them, and they had to crane their necks to see over the top. The gate was shut, so Thor went up and tried to open it.

They struggled with the gate for some time, and they couldn't get it to open, but then they found they could just squeeze through between the bars.

Inside the stronghold, they saw a great hall. The door was open, and they walked inside.

Games in Outgarth

There were benches down either side of the hall as far as the eye could see, and along the benches sat the etins, and most of them were giants.

Thor and his men made their way down to the king, Outgarth Loki, who was sitting on his high seat before the fire. They greeted him, but it was some time before he took any notice of them.

Then he flashed them his teeth in a grin and said, 'It's boring to hear about your long journey, but am I wrong or is this little chap the god Thor? I'm sure you must be bigger than you look. And what great deeds are there that you and your friends think you can manage? No one is allowed in here with us, unless they have some art or skill that sets them apart from other men.'

Loki had been lagging behind as they went into the hall, but now he called out, 'I have a skill which I'd be glad to prove. I can eat faster than anyone here!'

Outgarth Loki answered, 'That would be something if it turns out to be true, and we'll put your skill to the test.' He called down the benches to one of the etins, 'Logi, step out onto the floor and prove yourself against Loki.'

Then the king's men brought in a big wooden trough. They put it down in the middle of the floor and filled it with meat. Loki sat at one end and Logi at the other, and they both started eating their way as fast as they could along the trough. They came face to face right in the middle, and looked at what they had eaten.

Loki had eaten all the meat off the bones and stripped them bare, but Logi had eaten not just the meat but the bones as well and also the trough. So it seemed that Loki had lost that game.

'We'll have another game,' said Outgarth Loki, 'and see if someone else has a skill. What can this boy do?'

Thialfi said, 'Back home, everyone thought I was a good runner. I'll prove myself in a race against whoever you can find.'

'Now, that's a real skill,' said Outgarth Loki, 'but you'll have to be quick if you want to win here. We'll try you out straightaway.'

He took them outside, where there was a good flat running track. Then he called out to a little boy called Hugi, and asked him to run against Thialfi.

They set off together in the first race, but by the end Hugi was so far in front that he ran back to meet Thialfi.

Outgarth Loki said, 'You'll have to try harder, Thialfi, if you want to win. But it's true that I've never seen anyone come here who can run better than you.'

Then they tried another race, but when Hugi came to the finish and turned back, Thialfi was still a long way behind. Then Outgarth Loki said, 'Thialfi ran well, but I don't think he's going to win the game. Let's see what happens when they run the third race.'

They had one more race. This time, when Hugi ran to the finish and turned round, Thialfi had only got half way along the track. Then everyone agreed the game was over.

'Very well then, Thor,' said Outgarth Loki, 'We have all heard about your mighty deeds. What great feat will you show us now?'

Thor said, 'I'd be happy to have a drinking match with anyone here.'

Outgarth Loki turned to his cup bearer and said, 'Bring in the drinking horn that my men use!' The cup bearer came back with a horn and handed it to Thor. Then Outgarth Loki said, 'With this horn we say it's "Well drunk!" if you drink it off in one go. Some people might take two goes to drain it, but there's no one here who can't drain it in three.'

Thor looked at the horn. It was quite long but it didn't seem too big, and he was very thirsty. He tipped his head back and started to drink. He took great gulps, and he thought he'd empty the horn in one go. But when he ran out of breath and straightened his neck to look into the horn, it seemed that hardly a drop had gone.

'A good drink,' said Outgarth Loki, 'but not a very big one. It's hard to believe that the god Thor would not drink more than that. But of course, I'm sure you mean to finish it with your next drink.'

Thor didn't answer. He put the horn to his lips, and he thought that this time he'd take a bigger drink. He struggled to drink as long as he had breath, and he drank much longer this time.

But when he took the horn away from his mouth and looked inside, it seemed to have gone down less than before. So far, he had drunk just enough so you could carry the horn without spilling it.

Outgarth Loki said, 'What's up, Thor? You've left rather a lot there for your last drink. If you're going to finish it now, the third drink will have to be the biggest. We can't treat you as the great man they say you are, unless you do better in the other games than in this one.'

Then Thor got angry. He put the horn to his lips and drank as deep as he could, and he struggled longer than ever with the drink. When he looked in the horn, it seemed only a little bit lower than before.

'I won't drink any more,' said Thor, and he gave the horn back.

Then Outgarth Loki said, 'It's easy to see now, that you're not quite as mighty as we thought. Would you like to try another game? You're not much good at this one.'

'I could try another game,' said Thor, 'but no one would call those small drinks if I were back home with the gods. Anyway, what game have you got for me now?'

Outgarth Loki looked at Thor with a smile on his lips. 'The little boys here like to pick up my cat,' he said. 'Of course, it's not much of a feat, but it seems you're not as strong as we'd thought.'

Just then, a grey cat jumped onto the hall floor, and it was rather a big one. Thor went up and put his hands underneath its belly and lifted it up. But the cat arched its back as Thor raised his hands, so that even when Thor held it up as high as he could reach, the cat only had to lift one foot off the floor.

Thor couldn't do any more in that game.

Then Outgarth Loki said, 'This game has worked out just as I thought it would. The cat's rather big, and Thor is only little beside the big men we have here.'

'So I'm "little" am I?' said Thor. 'Well, let anyone try to wrestle with me now I'm angry!'

Then Outgarth Loki answered, and he looked down the benches. 'I don't see anyone here who would think it worth their while to wrestle with you,' he said. 'But wait! Call in my old nurse Elli, and Thor can wrestle with her if he wants. She has brought down men who didn't look any weaker than Thor.'

An old woman hobbled slowly into the hall. They spread a cloak on the floor for them to wrestle on. But when Elli took Thor in the wrestling hold, her grip was like iron. They wrestled together for a while, and the more Thor struggled against her, the firmer she stood.

Then the old woman tried some tricks, and Thor lost his footing so that he went down on one knee. She couldn't throw him to the ground, but Thor couldn't get up.

Outgarth Loki went over and told them to stop, and he said there was no need for Thor to wrestle with anyone else. By then it was late in the evening, and Outgarth Loki showed Thor and his men to their seats in the hall. They spent the night there, and they were well looked after.

In the morning, Thor and his men got up and dressed at dawn. They were ready to go, when Outgarth Loki came over and had a table laid with a hearty breakfast for them, and plenty to eat and drink.

When they had eaten, they went on their way.

Outgarth Loki went with them out of the stronghold and, when they said goodbye he turned to Thor and said, 'So, what did you think of your trip to Outgarth, Thor? Have you ever met anyone as mighty as me?'

'All I have earned here is shame and sorrow,' said Thor. 'And I have learned that you can call me a little man to my face, and I don't like that.'

Outgarth Loki said, 'I'll tell you the truth now, because you're outside the stronghold. Nothing has been quite what it seemed since you came to Outgarth, and there is all manner of trickery around my stronghold.

'You see me now as Outgarth Loki, but I was also the etin Skrymir who you met in the woods, and I tied your bag with iron wire so you could never have undone it unless you knew.

'It was the same with the games. Loki went first, and he tried to out-eat Logi. He was very hungry and he ate fast, but Logi means "Flame" and he is wildfire, so he burned through the trough just as fast as through the meat.

'Thialfi ran a race with someone called Hugi, but Hugi means "Thought", and he couldn't hope to run faster than Thought itself.

'But those,' said Outgarth Loki, 'were little things. It was when Thor started his games that we saw how strong the gods can be. When you were drinking from the horn and you thought it was going slowly, you didn't see that the other end of the horn was out in the sea. But you drank so much, that the water was pulled right back from the shore.'

That's what people call the ebb tide today.

Outgarth Loki said more. 'It was your next deed that shocked us most, because the cat you lifted up was not what you thought. It was the Midgarth Snake that lies wrapped around the Earth with its tail gripped in its teeth. But when you lifted it up, it was barely long enough for both its head and tail to touch the ground, and you held it so high that you nearly touched the sky.

'It was also a wonder that you lasted so long in the wrestling and only went down on one knee, because you were wrestling against Elli, who is Old Age. There has never been anyone, nor ever will be, who is not thrown to the ground by Old Age if he lives long enough, yet you only went down on one knee.

'Now it is time for us to part, and if I have my way, you will never find the path back to my hall again. Indeed, you'd never have got in at all, if I had known how strong you really were. I shall always keep my stronghold hidden with such tricks or with others, so you can never get the better of me.'

Thor's hand was on his hammer, and he was thinking of pulling it out and smashing this etin on the head, but there was something he still wanted to know.

'When I hit you on the head,' he said, 'how come it didn't kill you?'

'You never hit me on the head, Thor,' said Outgarth Loki. 'You see that flat-topped mountain above my hall, with the three square valleys in it, one deeper than the rest; those are your hammer marks. I put the hill between me and your hammer blows, but you never saw that.'

When Thor heard this, he grabbed his hammer and swung it up, but Outgarth Loki was gone and he couldn't see him anywhere. He turned round towards Outgarth to smash the stronghold, but he saw only broad green fields and there was no stronghold there.

Then he turned round again, and trudged back home to Strength Field with Thialfi. But Loki stayed behind in Etinhome.

Aegir's Brewpot

The sea etin Aegir came to Asgarth for the feast of Winter's Eve, and he was treated as an honoured guest. In the evening when it was time for drinking, Odin had swords brought into the hall and they shone so bright that no other lights were needed. Each of the gods sat in a high seat, and the walls were hung with painted shields.

The gods served Aegir with beer out of Thor's own drinking bowls. But for all the splendours of Asgarth, Aegir told wonderful stories of his hall beneath the waves, of the great feasts he held there and of the many men who sat around his benches. 'My hall is even bigger,' he said, 'than Thor's hall of Thunder Flash!'

It was then that Thor came back from Outgarth. He walked into Bright Home, and he saw the big sea etin Aegir with his green beard sitting in the seat of honour, drinking from his bowls.

'What is this etin doing at our feast?' said Thor. 'I have come back from Etinhome, where I did great deeds but was met with scorn and mockery. Logi Forniot's son was there in Outgarth, and he took part in their trickery. Yet his brother Aegir sits here boasting, and does nothing to prove himself.'

Odin said, 'Welcome, Thor. We miss you at our feasts. Tell us news of your long journey. What deeds have you done in Etinhome?'

'I drank and ate with the etins in Outgarth. I was stronger than them all, but still I was made a laughing stock.'

'But tell us, Thor,' said Odin, 'did you not show your strength at fighting or wrestling when you were in Outgarth?'

'I did wrestle there, against Old Age herself, who throws everyone to the floor. I alone stood strong against her, but yet there was no winner.'

Aegir said, 'I think you'd do badly against Earth's Belt, if you can't beat an old woman.'

'I lifted the Great Monster, that hideous serpent hateful to gods and men, from the floor of the sea. And yet I was tricked, so I could not overthrow it.'

'Midgarth's Snake got the better of you,' said Aegir, 'and I don't think there are many who could overcome the Serpent of the Seas.'

'If we met again in a fair fight,' said Thor, 'then I'd finish him!'

'I think your powers are no match for the might of the deep,' said Aegir, 'and you'd not be so strong on the sea.'

'I drank so deep from Outgarth's horn, that I drained the sea half dry!'

All Father said, 'My friends, our feast is almost done, and winter is nearly upon us. Who among us will feast us all for Yule at midwinter?'

Thor looked Aegir hard in the eye. He said, 'Aegir is drinking the beer of the gods. He boasts that his hall has longer benches, and that he holds greater feasts. Let Aegir feast us for Yule this year and every year at midwinter!'

'You've already tasted too much of my beer,' said Aegir, 'when you drank so much of the sea. There's no pot big enough to make beer for you all. If you want to drink my beer again, you must get me a kettle to brew it in.'

No one was more worried about this than Thor.

'Where could we get such a kettle?' he asked.

Tyr said, 'My father Hymir in Etinhome has the biggest brewpot you could believe, an iron kettle a mile wide.'

'Those etins played tricks on me,' said Thor. 'We'll get them back, if we think of a trick to get that kettle.'

So Thor dressed himself up as a young lad and gave himself the name of Warden. He took Tyr with him and set out for Hymir's house in Etinhome. His goat was still lame, so they went by foot. They travelled across Midgarth without goats or wagon, and reached the house at nightfall.

Tyr's grandmother opened the door to them. First one head peered around the door, then another, and then another, because Tyr's etin grandmother had plenty of heads - nine hundred in all!

Then Tyr's mother came out. Her name was Hroth and she was as lovely as the other was hideous. She greeted them kindly and brought them beer.

'You're very welcome here,' said Hroth, 'but hide yourselves up in the pots overhead, because my husband Hymir can often be unfriendly when he gets home.'

There were nine pots hanging from the roof beam of the house, and Tyr and Thor hid themselves in the biggest. They waited there until long after dark, when the etin Hymir came home from his hunting. The snow lay thick on his shoulders, and his beard tinkled with clattering icicles as he strode scowling into the hall.

His wife stepped up and said, 'Welcome home, Hymir. Cheer up, now! Your own son Tyr has come home to see you, and his friend Warden is with him.'

The etin stared angrily around the hall, looking for his unwelcome guests. He caught sight of the roof beam where the pots were hanging, and his stare was so hard that the beam split in two, and the pots came crashing to the floor. Eight were broken into pieces. Only one stayed whole, the great iron kettle where the gods had hidden.

Thor and Tyr stepped out, but Hymir's heart didn't jump for joy when he saw his two guests on the floor before him.

'I'll need to keep an eye on that lad, Warden,' the etin muttered. Then he said, 'Kill three of my bulls, to cook for our supper. I reckon we'll need plenty of meat tonight.'

The bulls were slaughtered and set to boil. When the meat was cooked, they sat down to dinner. Thor had soon munched his way through one of the bulls, so he helped himself to the next.

Hymir was watching Thor angrily and he said, 'Tomorrow, I think we'll find our own food, so there might be enough to go round.'

'That's a good idea,' said Thor. 'Let's go fishing together!'

Hymir said, 'I can't see what use you'd be in the boat, so little and puny as you look. And you'll whine with cold if I go out as far and stay out as long as I usually do.'

'We've yet to see who'll be the first to whine for home,' said Thor, 'and I say we should play a game. Whoever can prove he is stronger and bolder can take whatever he wants as his own, and I'll have that big brewpot we were sitting in.'

'This is child's play,' said the etin. 'A young lad like you could never beat an old etin like me, and I think I'll brew beer in my own kettle again just as before.'

Next morning, Hymir was up and dressed before dawn, and Thor wasn't far behind him. They set off down by the cliff, to where Hymir's fishing boat lay moored in the cove below.

Thor said, 'What'll we do for bait?'

'I've got my bait,' said Hymir. 'You get your own!'

So Thor went into the field where Hymir's cattle were. There was a great black bull there called Heaven Springer. Thor took it by the horns and twisted until the head came off. He took that down the cliff to Hymir's boat.

'I've got bait now too,' said Thor.

Hymir looked at the head of his best bull lying in the boat and frowned. 'Your handiwork today is no better than your table manners last night,' he said.

They took up the oars and started to row. The etin thought Warden's rowing was pretty strong, and it wasn't long before Hymir said, 'We can stop now. I have caught a lot of plaice and flounders and other flatfish here.'

'No,' said Thor. 'We'll row on out.'

After a while Hymir said, 'We'll have to stop now, or we'll reach the deepest Ocean where the Great Monster lurks.'

But again Thor said, 'No. We'll row on out.'

He rowed on until Hymir said, 'Now we have reached the deepest Ocean, where the Midgarth Serpent can get us.'

Then Thor brought his oars in, and laid them down inside the boat. Hymir got to work chopping up bait with his long, sharp knife. He set the bait on his hooks, and dropped his fishing lines overboard. It wasn't long before Hymir was hauling in whales on all his hooks, and throwing them down in the boat like flatfish.

Thor had a good stout rope for his fishing line, and he tied a big iron spike onto it. He took the head of the bull Heaven Springer, and set that onto the spike. Then he dropped it over the side of the boat, and let the rope slip through his hands as the bait sank down and down into the depths of the sea.

Down below at the bottom of the ocean, the Great Monster smelled blood in the water and turned his head to look. He saw the bull's head, he stretched his great mouth wide, and he bit. Then the iron spike stuck through the roof of the serpent's mouth, and he was hooked on the line.

Up above, Storm Rider felt the tug on the rope when the Great Monster bit, and he started to pull in his catch. Slowly, he hauled the Midgarth Serpent up from the depths. But as he was pulling, the snake gave a sudden jerk with its neck and yanked on the rope, so that Thor's fists banged down hard on the side of the boat and he skinned his hands along the top strake.

Then Thor got angry, and he used all his god-strength. He pushed his feet down through the bottom of the boat, so he was standing on the bed of the ocean. Thor heaved

126

on the rope, while Hymir sat trembling with fright as he stared at the sea washing in and out of his boat, and at Thor pulling the huge monster out of the deep.

Thor hauled that serpent up and up, until at last the head broke through the waves. And it's true to say that you've never seen a dreadful sight, unless you were there and saw that monstrous skull coming out of sea, or saw how Thor fixed his eyes on it, and how the serpent stared back at him spitting poison.

Thor brought his hammer up to strike, and he was just about to hurl it. But as the monster's head came up from the water, the colour drained from Hymir's face and he went deathly white. He looked at the monster's foul head and at the waves surging into the boat, and he panicked.

Just as Thor was raising his hammer to strike, Hymir reached for his bait knife, leaned forward and hacked through the rope.

Then the serpent's great head sank back beneath the water. Thor threw his hammer after it, and there was a screech from under the waves as it hit the monster's head. The whole earth echoed with the roar that rose from beneath the sea.

Some people say that Thor's hammer struck off the serpent's head and that the Great Monster died there, but many believe it is living still and that one day it will meet Thor again at the Doom of the Powers.

Hymir was silent and stony-faced as they rowed home.

'I rowed us out to the deepest ocean,' said Thor. 'I hooked the Great Monster and there's no bigger fish than that, so I win the game!'

But Hymir said, 'Well, I don't see that you've been much use today. I caught six whales for us to eat tonight, but you've caught nothing at all. It's true you can row well enough, but that won't win the pot. So, if you want to stay, you'll have to do your share of the work. Either you carry our catch back to the house, or else you can tie up the boat.'

Then Thor picked up the boat with the whales still in it and all the water that had washed over the decks. He carried it up the cliff face and threw it down at Hymir's door.

'Now do you see that I'm stronger than you?' he said. 'I win the game and the pot is mine.'

But Hymir said, 'The pot is still mine. It might be true that you've got some strength, but you won't be strong enough to win unless you can break my wineglass.'

Hymir's wineglass looked easy to break, so Thor threw it down hard on the floor. There was a hole in the floor where it landed, but the wineglass was unbroken.

Then he threw it against one of the hall pillars. The pillar snapped in two and a beam fell from the roof, but the glass was still unbroken. Storm Rider was reaching for his hammer, when Tyr's mother whispered in his ear.

'You'll never break that glass,' she said, 'unless it hits the only thing that's stronger than it. Hymir's head is made of stone. Throw it against the old etin's head, and then it will smash into pieces.'

Thor jumped up on Hymir's knee and brought the cup down on his head. When the glass struck the etin's stone skull, it shattered into pieces and the pieces fell onto Hymir's knees.

The etin looked down at the broken shards which lay in his lap and he said, 'I know that I have lost a lot, when I see the glass lying broken in my lap. I'll never again be able to say, "Beer, you are brewed!" The pot is yours, if you can move it.'

Tyr said he'd try to move it, but no matter how hard he pushed, it wouldn't budge. Then Thor picked up the pot and put it on his head. He and Tyr set off for home, with the pot chains jangling around Thor's heels.

They hadn't reached the edge of Etinhome, before they heard an army of etins coming after them. Thor had to stop and put the kettle down, to kill them all with his hammer. Then he picked up the pot again, and carried it off to Aegir's hall.

The Fight with Hrungnir

Thor was still off fishing with Hymir, when Odin saddled his horse Slider and put on his golden helm, and he rode like the wind as far as Etinhome.

The etin Hrungnir was watching from his hall door at Gritgarth, and he called out, 'Who is this man with the golden helm who can ride over sea and sky? It's a good horse that can manage that!'

All Father drew in his reins and rode over to Hrungnir. 'Slider is the best of horses,' he said, 'and there isn't a horse to match him in all Etinhome!'

'It's a good horse indeed,' said Hrungnir, 'but I have the horse that will beat him, and he's called Gold Mane.'

Odin took one look at the etin's horse and said, 'He's no match for Slider.'

He set his heels to his horse's sides and away he sped.

Then Hrungnir got angry, and he thought he'd teach Odin a lesson for his boasting. So he leapt on his horse's back and galloped off after him.

Odin rode so hard that he was already over the skyline and out of sight. But Hrungnir was in such an etin mood that he rode all the way to Asgarth before he knew where he was, and right in through the gates of the gods. It was only when he saw Odin's home Kill Hall in front of him that he stopped.

There are five hundred and forty doors in that hall, and each door is wide enough for eight hundred men to walk through side-by-side. The whole of the roof is tiled with war-shields. There is a wolf hanging above the west door, and an eagle flying over the end gable. When Hrungnir came to the hall doors, the gods asked him in for a drink, so he walked inside.

There are countless benches in that hall, where the Lone Warriors sit every evening for their feast. The rafters which hold up the roof are made from spear shafts, and there are iron shirts strewn on the benches. Hrungnir saw All Father's high seat of Lid Shelf, and another high seat on the far side of the hall. He sat down there and called out for drink.

The gods brought out the drinking bowls that Thor would use. They filled them with beer and brought them to Hrungnir. He took them and drained them both.

Then he called for more. And when Hymir got drunk, he had plenty of big words to say to the gods.

He said, 'I'm going to pick up Kill Hall, and I'll take it back to Etinhome. I'm going to kill all the gods - all except Freya and Sif, and they can come home with me. And as for the walls of Asgarth, I'll bury them deep under the earth.'

And so he went on, and still he called for more beer. But only Freya still dared to fetch him drink.

'I like you, Freya,' said Hrungnir. 'You can come home with me. But first, I'm going to drink all the beer in Asgarth!'

When the gods were tired of his boasting, they spoke the name of Thor. As soon as they had uttered his name, there stood Thor in the middle of the hall and he stepped up to the etin with his hammer raised.

'Who has let this cunning etin come into the hall of the gods?' he bellowed. 'And why is Freya bringing him drink, as if he's a guest at our feast?'

Hrungnir looked at Thor, and his eyes were not friendly. He said, 'It was Odin who asked me to sit in his hall, and it was Odin who offered me drink.'

'You'll be sorry for that before you leave here,' said Thor.

But Hrungnir said, 'It's a pity I left my weapons at home, my shield and my whetstone, and if I had them here there'd be some fighting now. But it would do you no honour to kill me when I'm unarmed and weaponless. So I challenge you, Thor, to meet me tomorrow at Gritgarth for a duel.'

Then Thor smiled. No one had ever dared challenge him to a duel before. Hrungnir got up on Gold Mane, and he galloped off to Etinhome to tell the etins what he had done.

Soon all the etins were talking about Hrungnir's duel. It mattered a lot to them that Hrungnir should win, because he was the strongest among the etins, and Thor was their greatest enemy. So if Hrungnir lost the fight, they'd have little good to look forward to from Thor.

By the rules of the duel, each of them had to bring someone to stand by him as his second in the fight. Thor chose the boy Thialfi as his second, but none of the etins was keen to face Thor in a duel. So they gathered on the fields of Gritgarth, to make a new etin out of earth for the fight against Thor.

They made him nine miles high and three miles broad. Then they wondered where to get a heart big enough for him, but they took the heart out of a mare and put that into the new etin's breast. It started to beat and the etin got up. They gave him the name of Cloud Legs, and he was the biggest etin there has been since the days of Ymir. But it is said that the mare's heart inside him skipped a beat, when Cloud Legs saw Thor coming.

Hrungnir's heart was made of stone with three spikes on it, and his head too was made of stone. He had a big stone shield, broad and thick, which he held out in front of him as he waited at Gritgarth, and a big whetstone which he carried as a club over his shoulder. He wasn't a pretty sight. Behind him stood Cloud Legs, who was already scared witless.

Then Thor's lad Thialfi came running up and said, 'You're in for it now, etin, because Thor has seen you standing there with your shield held high, so he's coming by the lower road.'

And he pointed at the ground.

Hrungnir dropped his shield to the ground and stood on it. Then the lightning flashed and thunder sounded through the skies. Hrungnir looked up and he saw Thor above him with his hammer. He was driving his wagon with the two goats Tooth Gnasher and Tooth Grinder out in front, and they came hurtling towards him.

Hrungnir took his whetstone club in both hands and hurled it at Thor, and when Thor saw the club coming towards him, he threw his hammer. The two weapons met in mid-air with the sound of a thunderclap.

Hrungnir's club was shattered, and pieces of whetstone were scattered all over the fields of Gritgarth. But one lump whizzed on through the air, and hit Thor in the middle of his forehead. It knocked him straight out of his wagon onto the ground.

Thor's hammer flew on, until it struck Hrungnir's stone skull and smashed it to pieces. The etin fell flat on his back, with one leg on top of Thor's neck, pinning him to the ground.

Thor lay there under the etin's leg. He felt dizzy and his head was sore. He looked at Thialfi, who was digging in the mud with a spade. 'What are you doing?' asked Thor.

'I'm fighting the other etin!' said Thialfi. 'Cloud Legs was so scared when he saw you, that he wet himself. And because he was made of earth, he turned into a pile of mud. Now I'm fighting him with my spade.'

'Come and get me out of here!' said Thor.

Then Thialfi went over to help Thor get up. He tried to lift the etin's leg, but it wouldn't budge.

When the gods heard that Thor was down, they all came to help. But not one of them could shift Hrungnir's leg.

Then Thor's son Magni toddled up. He was just three years old, but he flung the etin's leg off with one hand.

'Daddy,' he said, 'what a pity I wasn't here before, because I think I could have knocked this etin flat with one punch from my fist!'

Thor gave him a big hug. 'You'll be a fine strong chap when you grow up,' he said, 'and I'm going to give you that etin's horse, Gold Mane, as a present.'

Odin said, 'It's not right to give such a fine horse to the son of an etin girl, instead of to your own father!'

Magni's mother was the etin Ironknife, but that didn't stop Thor from giving him the horse.

Thor went home to Strength Field, but he still had a lump of stone stuck in his head. Then the witch Groa came to Thor's hall. Groa was the wife of the etin-killer Aurvandil the Bold, and she knew the spells to get that stone out of Thor's head. She chanted her spells over Thor, until the whetstone began to loosen in his forehead.

When Thor felt the stone loosen, he was so pleased that he wanted to say something to make her happy. He said, 'I've got good news for you, because when I was coming back from Etinhome, I met your husband Aurvandil, and he was trying to get home. So I picked him up and put him in a basket on my back, and I carried him south as I waded through the floods of Sleet Waves.

'One of his toes was sticking out of the basket,' said Thor, 'and it was so cold there, that by the time we got across Sleet Waves it had frozen solid. So I snapped it off and I threw it up into the sky to make a star.' That star can still be seen to this day, and it is called Aurvandil's Toe.

'So anyway,' said Thor, 'it won't be long now before he gets home.'

But Groa was so happy when she heard this news, that she completely forgot her spells. So the whetstone never came out, and it is still stuck in Thor's forehead now.

That's why there's something you should never do: Never throw a whetstone inside a house, because then the stone moves in Thor's forehead, and it hurts.

Peace with Geirrod

Loki had borrowed Freya's hawk-skin and was out flying for the fun of it in Etinhome. He had flown into Geirrod's Garth, and he saw a big hall there built into the mountainside. He wanted to have a closer look, so he landed at one of the windows and looked inside.

There were lots of etins along the benches, and they were feasting noisily. But Geirrod looked up and saw him there.

'Fetch that hawk,' he said, 'and bring it to me!'

Straightaway, one of his men began to climb as fast as he dared up the wall to where Loki was perched. It was a tough climb, and it was a long way up.

Loki was pleased to see how hard it was for Geirrod's man to climb up to get him, and he thought it would be funny to stay there and fly off at the last moment, so that the man would have to struggle all the way to the top for nothing.

He watched him make his way up, and when the man got within reach and made a grab for him, Loki flapped his wings and tried to take off, but he found his feet were stuck and he couldn't fly. So Loki was caught, and he was taken down to the etin Geirrod.

Geirrod looked hard at the hawk and said, 'These are a hawk's feathers, but these are not a hawk's eyes. Speak to us, hawk, and tell us who you are, and what you are doing here!'

But Loki said nothing.

'Bird or man, I will make you speak,' said Geirrod. He took the hawk to an iron chest, opened the lid and put it inside. 'There you will stay without food or drink until you talk.'

For three long months, Loki was locked in that chest. Every evening, he heard the etins feasting in the hall around him, while he was locked in the darkness with nothing to eat or drink. But at the end of three months, the lid opened and Geirrod took him out.

'Now, hawk,' said the etin, 'tell us who you are, and what you are doing here!'

'I am Loki, the Aesir's messenger,' said Loki. 'I am flying over Etinhome to get news for the gods.'

'A messenger from the gods, are you?' said Geirrod with a grin. 'Then, bird, you shall eat, if you will give me your solemn vow that you will send Thor here to me without his goats and his wagon, without his iron gloves or his belt of strength, and without his hammer.'

Loki gave his solemn promise that he would do that, and then Geirrod let him eat.

When he got back to Asgarth, Loki said to Thor, 'There are green fields around Geirrod's hall, and broad roads will lead you there. Of all etins, he is the most welcoming. I spent three months in his hall, and plenty of food was served there. Geirrod wants to make peace between gods and etins, and he wants to give you his warmest welcome.'

'I'd rather go ready for battle,' said Thor.

'No,' said Loki. 'You must go in good faith, without threats and without weapons or armour. Then you will do what has never been done, and make peace for ever throughout the Nine Worlds.'

So Thor set off on foot with his lad Thialfi, while Loki flew off to tell Geirrod. They walked all day over moors and mountains until they came to the house of the etin woman Grid, who was the mother of Odin's son Vidar the Silent. They stayed there for the night, and she asked them where they were going. They told her they were off to Geirrod's hall, to make peace between gods and etins.

'I think Loki has been lying to you,' said Grid. 'Geirrod is a cunning etin and very hard to deal with. There's no one crueller in all Etinhome, unless it's his dreadful daughters. They give no peace to the etins, and they'll give none to the gods.'

Thor looked downcast at this news.

'We have promised in good faith that we'll go,' he said, 'so we have to go on.'

Grid asked if they had any armour or weapons with them, and said she'd lend Thor her iron gloves and her belt of strength, and also her iron rod. She looked after the gods well that night, and in the morning they set off for Geirrod's Garth with the things she had lent them.

There is a river in Etinhome called Dizziness that plunges between steep mountains. It is the greatest of all rivers. When Thor came to the bank he buckled on the belt of strength and, with Grid's rod to steady himself, he started to wade out into the rushing river.

Thialfi grabbed hold of Thor's belt at the back, and he clung on for dear life.

But when they were halfway across, the waters started to rise up around them, so that Thor nearly lost his footing on the slippery rocks, and the stream gushed over his shoulders. Thor leaned heavily on Grid's rod and said, 'Either these waters must sink, or my god strength must rise right up to the skies.'

Then Thor looked up to the source of the river, and he saw an etin woman squatting over it with one foot on each bank, making water in the river and making it rise. It was Geirrod's daughter Yelp.

'Stop a stream where it starts,' said Thor. He picked up a big stone from the river bed and lobbed it at her.

He didn't miss, and the water started to go down.

Thor found he was near the bank, so he grabbed hold of a rowan tree to pull himself out, and he clambered up onto the bank. That is why the rowan is known as 'Thor's Help'.

There was a crowd of many-headed etins in the mountains above, and they started to hurl rocks down on the gods. But Thor caught every stone and hurled it back against them, until so many were dead that the rest turned and fled in terror.

Then they went on to Geirrod's Garth.

The etins met them at the gate and showed them to a goat shed. 'Get in there!' they said. 'That's where you'll stay until Geirrod wants to meet you.'

Thor and Thialfi went into the goat shed. There were no goats inside, just a single stone seat. It was Thor who sat down.

But as he sat down, Thor felt the seat lift off the floor beneath him, and he found his head up among the iron rafters. Just before he was crushed against the stone ceiling, Thor shoved Grid's rod into the rafters and pushed himself back down to the ground.

There was a hideous crack and a ghastly scream underneath him.

When Thor looked under the seat, he saw the bodies of Geirrod's two daughters, Yelp and Grip. They had tried to crush him to death against the ceiling, but Thor had broken their backs when he pushed down with Grid's rod.

'This peace is not very peaceable,' said Thor.

Then he got up, and strode straight into Geirrod's hall in the mountain.

There were fires burning all down the middle of the hall with great iron pillars between them, and there were iron benches all along the sides, with etins drinking and eating at every bench. Thor saw Geirrod standing behind the biggest fire with a pair of tongs in his hand and the fire blazing up before him.

'Come and share our feast with us, Thor,' said Geirrod. 'Hot metal fresh from the fire!' He pulled a glowing lump of red hot iron out of the flames with his tongs, and he threw it hard at Thor.

Thor reached out and caught the molten metal in the iron glove. Then Geirrod hid behind a pillar, as Thor raised the molten ingot in the air and flung it right through the pillar and through the etin too, through the rock wall behind him and on into the ground outside.

So Geirrod was killed and his hall crumbled around him, crushing all the etins beneath the mountain.

That is how Thor made peace with Geirrod.

Balder's Death

Frigg is the queen of the gods. She lives at Fen Hall and her husband is Odin. She had three sons called Hermod, Hoder and Balder. Balder was the eldest. Of all the gods, he was the most beautiful. His voice was soft, and his words were gentle and kind.

Everybody loved and trusted Balder, not only gods and people but even etins and trolls, because he was always fair-minded and even-handed in his words and judgements.

Balder lived at Broad Gleam where there is nothing that is unclean. And his wife Nanna, Nep's daughter, was just as good and kind-hearted as he was himself. Their son is called Forseti, and he can solve all arguments.

But Balder had bad dreams. He dreamt that he was going to die.

Gods do not die. They eat the Apples of Life which keep them forever young, and they never grow old. But Balder dreamt he would die, so Frigg called upon everything to swear a vow not to harm Balder.

She took oaths from fire and water, from iron and other metals, from stones and earth, from trees and plants, from birds and animals, from sicknesses, from poisons and from snakes, that they would not harm him. They all swore gladly, because of the love they had for Balder.

After that, the gods found a new game to play.

Balder would stand on the grass of Ida Field, and the gods stood all around him in a ring, throwing things and trying to hit him. Some of them threw spears, some struck at him with weapons, and the rest threw stones. But no matter what they did to him, Balder was never hurt.

Everyone was calling out and laughing at the game, because whatever they tried to hit him with would stop short and would not harm him, even if they walked right up to Balder and struck him with a sword.

Loki thought the gods looked very pleased with themselves, so he turned himself into an old woman, and he hobbled away to Fen Hall to speak to Frigg. There the old woman said, 'I have been far and seen many things, but never have I seen the like of what I saw today. All the gods are throwing things at Balder, yet nothing will harm him. How can this be?'

148

'No weapons nor trees, no metals nor stones will harm Balder.' said Frigg, 'I have taken an oath from each of them.'

The old woman said, 'Has everything sworn the oath to spare Balder?'

And Frigg said, 'There is a twig growing on a tree to the west of Kill Hall. It is called Mistletoe, and it was too young to take the oath.'

At that the old woman vanished, and she was nowhere to be seen.

Loki went straight to that tree west of Kill Hall, and cut himself a sprig of mistletoe. He sharpened it, and took it back to where the gods were still throwing things at Balder.

There was one god there who was standing apart from the ring of gods around Balder. It was Balder's brother, blind Hoder. Loki went up to him and put his hand on his shoulder. 'Hoder,' he said, 'why don't you join in the fun, and honour Balder like the other men?'

Hoder said, 'Loki, I am blind. I can't see where to strike.'

'You're always on the outside, while your brother Balder is right in the middle. Everyone is looking at him, and they see you no more than you can see them. But I will be your eyes,' said Loki, 'and I will tell you where to strike.'

Hoder said, 'It was always Balder that everyone loved. But anyway, I haven't got a weapon.'

'Take this twig,' said Loki. 'It is called Mistletoe. It will make you more powerful than Balder, and with it you will strike a blow that will long be remembered among gods and men.'

Hoder took the mistletoe. He stepped forward and struck Balder, so that the mistletoe went right through him, and he fell dead.

Suddenly everything was silent.

The gods were struck dumb. Nobody moved, not even to lift Balder from the ground where he lay. They looked at each other, and everyone wanted to strike down Balder's killer, but they knew it was forbidden to spill blood in this holy place. And nobody could speak. And when they did try to speak it was only crying that came out, and they could not tell each other in words about the grief and the sorrow they felt.

That was how Balder died, and it was the unhappiest deed ever done amongst gods or men.

After Loki had done this, he ran off and hid from the gods. His shoes took him over sea and sky, and he made his home in a cave on a steep mountain.

The gods held a funeral for Balder, to send him on his way to Shadow Home where Hel rules over the dead. Balder's ship was called Ring Horn. It was the biggest of ships, and it stood on rollers by the shore ready to be launched. The gods chose it to be his funeral ship. They took Balder's body down to the ship, and lit a great fire there.

All of the gods gathered by the funeral ship: Odin was on his eight-legged horse Slider, and with him was his wife Frigg, and his valkyries and ravens; Thor was in his wagon drawn by the two goats Tooth Gnasher and Tooth Grinder; Frey was in a cart drawn by the boar Golden Bristle; his sister Freya rode in her wagon drawn by two great cats; Heimdal rode a horse called Gold Tuft; and there were lots of frost etins there too, as well as mountain etins.

Then Odin stooped and picked up the body of his son, and carried it up onto the ship. He bent over and whispered in Balder's ear, so that nobody else could hear what he said. But when Balder's wife Nanna watched his body carried onto the ship, her heart burst with grief and she died. The gods took her body and placed it beside Balder on the ship.

Each of the gods chose a gift for Balder, and laid it beside him in the ship. Odin gave him the arm ring Dripper, which had been given to him by the dwarf Brokk, and Frigg gave the finest of linen which she had woven herself. Balder's horse was led aboard too, with its saddle and bridle and all its harness.

Then none of the gods could move the ship into the water. But there was a troll woman there, and her name was Hyrrokin. She was riding on a wolf and she had snakes for reins. Hyrrokin jumped off her steed by the ship, and gave it a push with her hand. Flames shot out from the rollers and the whole earth shook as the ship slipped out into the sea.

They set light to the ship on the water there, and that is how Balder made his way down to Shadow Home, the world of death where Hel is queen.

After this, Odin spoke with Mimir's head, to learn who should take vengeance for Balder. Mimir said that the hand was still unborn that would take revenge, but that Billing's daughter Rinda would bear a son in Etinhome, a brother for Balder who would kill Balder's killer.

But Frigg wanted her son to come back to her. She called everyone together and she said, 'Who is there here who will win my blessing and my love, and will ride the road to Hel to find Balder, and offer her a ransom so he can come back again to Asgarth?'

Balder's brother Hermod stepped up and he said, 'I am bold enough to ride the road to Hel, and to find my brother in Shadow Home. I will offer her a ransom, if she will let him come home.'

Then Odin led out his horse Slider. Hermod got up on the horse, and he rode away.

He rode for nine long nights through dales so dark and deep that he saw nothing until he came to the River Yell, which lies at the edge of Shadow Home. There is a bridge across the river there that is covered with glittering gold, and it is called Yell's Bridge.

Beside the bridge was an etin woman called Modgud. As Hermod made his way across the bridge, she called out to him saying, 'Who are you, that you ride so heavily on Yell's Bridge? Five hundred souls have passed here with a lighter step, and you do not have the look of death. Why are you riding the road to Hel?'

He answered, 'My name is Hermod, Odin is my father. I am riding here to ask after Balder. Have you seen him here on the road to Hel?'

She said, 'It is nine long nights since Balder rode here over Yell's glittering Bridge, but downwards and northwards lies the road to Hel.'

Hermod rode on through Shadow Home until he came to Corpse Sands and to the high Gates of Hel, where she has her hall. Those gates will not open for the living, so Hermod spurred the horse on, and it leapt right over the top, and there is no other horse that would have taken that jump.

Beyond those gates, he saw a big ugly hall with its doors facing north. That is where Hel has her home, and it is called Sleet Fall. Its walls are made from snakes' backs and poison flows in streams throughout the hall.

Hermod rode right up to the door. He got off his horse and walked inside. There he saw Hel sitting on her high seat in the middle of the hall, and she was very dreadful to look at.

Across the hall on the other high seat sat his brother Balder. Between them was the fireplace, but any fire that once was there had burned out long ago, and it was cold and black. There was a plate beside the fireplace, and across the plate lay a knife. The plate's name is Hunger and it is always empty, and the knife is called Famine and it is very sharp.

Hermod stayed that night in Hel's hall of Sleet Fall, and there was little to eat and drink and not much laughter there. In the morning, he went up to where Hel sat on her high seat, and he dropped to his knees before her.

He said, 'There is only weeping in the world, because Balder has left us. We loved him better than anyone, and now everything is mourning his death. I beg you to let him come back among the living.'

Hel said, 'If it is true that Balder is so much loved and so much mourned, then I will allow him to leave me. So, if everything in the world, both living and dead will weep for him, then he may go back to join the gods in Asgarth. But if there is anyone that will not weep, then Balder shall stay here in Shadow Home with Hel.'

Hermod stood up, and Balder led him out of the hall. Then Balder took the ring Dripper from his arm and asked his brother to take it to Odin as a keepsake, and Nanna gave him a linen gown as a gift for Frigg and a gold ring for Frigg's maidservant Fulla.

Then Hermod rode back to Fen Hall in Asgarth, and he told Frigg everything that he had seen and heard in Shadow Home.

Frigg sent out her messenger Gna on her horse Hoof Thrower, to ride through all the Nine Worlds and to ask everything to weep Balder out of Hel.

Everything wept. All the people and animals, the trees and plants, the stones and earth, and every metal wept for Balder just as today, when the Sun warms them on a frosty morning, you may see them weeping still.

When Gna had done her work and was on her way home, she came to a cave door in a steep mountain which she had not seen before. There was an old etin woman sitting there by the fire, who said that her name was Thanks. Gna asked her to weep Balder out of Hel, but she said:

> Dry are the tears that Thanks will drop
> Over Balder's funeral pyre;
> Alive or dead, I little liked him;
> Hel can keep what she has.

So Balder must stay in Shadow Home still, and he has never gone back to the gods.

But many people think that the etin woman was Loki, Leafy's son.

Loki's Bickering

When it came to midwinter, the gods went to Aegir's hall beneath the waves at Leeward Isle. Aegir lives there with his wife Ran, and the gods went to drink the Yule beer, which Aegir had brewed in the huge kettle Thor brought from Hymir's hall.

Odin came to this feast, and Frigg his wife. Thor didn't go because he was off in Etinhome, but his wife Sif was there, and Bragi the Peacemaker with his wife Idun. One-handed Tyr was there too; the wolf Fenrir had bitten his other hand off when they bound him. Niord and Skadi were there together, as well as Frey and Freya, and Odin's son Vidar. There were very many gods and elves there.

There were also many men there who filled the benches of Aegir's hall, and all of them were sailors. Then the gods learned that Aegir's wife Ran has a net, which she casts up above the water and she catches ships and boats, and drags them down beneath the waves with their crewmen. These were the men who sat at the benches of Aegir's hall.

Loki turned up too. He had not shown his face in Asgarth since Balder's death, but now he came to join the gods in Aegir's hall.

Aegir had two serving men, called Fimafeng and Eldir. They had lit the hall with glittering gold instead of with firelight. The cooking fires too were glittering gold, and the food and the beer came in all by themselves.

The guests were full of praise for Aegir's serving men, and everything was calm and peaceful. But Loki couldn't stand that, so he killed Fimafeng.

The gods shook their shields and howled at Loki, and they drove him away to the woods. Then they started drinking again.

Loki went back to Leeward Isle, and he met Eldir outside the hall. 'What are the gods saying in there?' he asked.

'They're talking about their strength and their weapons,' said Eldir, 'and not one of them has a good word for you.'

'I think I'll go inside and stir things up a bit,' said Loki.

'You know if you stir the gods to anger, they'll wipe it off on you,' said Eldir.

'Don't get too clever, Eldir,' said Loki. 'You know I'll win any game of words.'

Then Loki went inside the hall. He looked around, and everything went quiet. All the gods looked at him.

'Well, I'm thirsty,' said Loki. 'I've come a long way to be here. Where shall I sit? Who'll get me a drink?'

'You have no place at the Aesir's feast,' said Bragi. 'The gods know best who they should drink with.'

Loki turned to where Odin sat in the high seat opposite Aegir. 'Have you forgotten, Odin, how once we mixed our blood together,' said Loki, 'and you said you'd never drink unless we drank together?'

'Get up then, Vidar,' said Odin, 'and make room for Loki. Let him sit down, so he won't speak ill of us in Aegir's hall.'

Vidar the Silent stood up and poured Loki a drink.

Loki raised his cup and drank a toast. 'Hail to the gods! Hail to the goddesses! Hail to the sacred powers – all except him over there, Bragi, who was so rude to me!'

Bragi said, 'Loki, I'll give you a horse and sword to keep you quiet. You can have a gold arm ring too, if you'll hold your tongue, and don't speak spiteful words to the gods.'

'Huh! You won't have much left to give, Bragi. You're never up for a fight. You just give it all away.'

'If we were outside now, I'd have your head off for that, you liar!' said Bragi.

'Don't blame him, Bragi,' said Idun. 'Remember he is one of the Aesir, and we must keep the peace among us.'

'You can shut up, Idun,' said Loki. 'You're so shameless that you kissed your brother's killer!'

'I'm not saying anything against you, Loki,' said Idun. 'I just don't want to see a fight.'

Odin said, 'You're mad, Loki, to talk like this, when the gods offer you friendship.'

'You can shut up, Odin. You never settle things fairly in battle; you often let cowards kill heroes. What sort of a war god is that?'

'Perhaps I have sometimes let cowards win, but you are the mother of my horse! What sort of a man is that?'

'Well, if I'm the mother of your horse, you will go round dressed up in woman's clothes like a witch. What sort of a man is that?'

Frigg said, 'If only Balder were here, he would know how to make peace even with you. His judgements were always fair.'

'Oh yes, Frigg,' said Loki, 'you might be right. But I have made sure that you'll never see Balder again in your halls.'

Freya said, 'You're mad, Loki, to count up your crimes. I think that Frigg sees more of the future than you would care to know.'

'You can shut up, Freya,' said Loki. 'You make a show of shutting your doors, but I found a way to your bed and took off your jewels!'

Tyr said, 'You're mad, Loki, to count up your crimes, but soon you will lie tied up in a cavern.'

'You can shut up, Tyr, you handless being! Fenrir has taken your best hand, so you won't be able to fight when the sons of Muspell come.'

Frey said, 'The wolf came off the worse, and is tied on an island in Utter Darkness. You'll soon be tied up too, unless you hold your tongue.'

'You can shut up, Frey. You bought your wife with gold, and gave away your sword. What will you fight with, when the sons of Muspell come?'

Sif said, 'Loki, take this glass of sweet mead. You know that I have never done wrong.'

'I remember, Sif, how I found you in bed and I held your hair in my hands. Thor was cheated by me then!'

'You have named him yourself,' said Sif. 'Now the mountains are shaking. I think Thor is here!'

Then Thor came in and he said, 'Shut up, Loki, or my hammer Miller will silence you! I'll knock your head off and end your life!'

'Listen to him!' said Loki. 'What a mood he's in. You'd hardly think he'd been cowering in the thumb of an etin's glove. He didn't look so big then.'

'Shut up, Loki, or my hammer Miller will silence you! With a single blow, I'll break every bone in your body.'

'You weren't so boastful, when Skrymir gave you his bag to open. You went hungry then because you couldn't undo it.'

'Shut up, Loki, or my hammer Miller will silence you! I'll send you to see your daughter Hel in Shadow Home.'

'I'd love to stay and talk some more,' said Loki, 'but it's time to go when Thor gets rough.'

Then he went outside and ran off.

After that, all the gods could talk about was how they were going to catch Loki. They knew he was cunning so they would have to be clever, and they agreed to take Kvasir with them, the wisest of men, to be their guide.

Loki's Binding

Loki ran off to the steep mountain, where he had built himself a house. Loki's house had four doors which were always open and he could see out on all sides, so he would see the gods no matter where they came from, and he could get out the other way.

There was a waterfall on the mountainside called Glinting, and under the waterfall was a deep pool and a river running down to the sea.

Loki sat by the fire in his house, and thought how he would outwit the gods. If they came to his house, he would go to the pool under the waterfall and take the shape of a salmon in the water. As a salmon, he would hide in the pool, and the gods would not be able to catch him.

So Loki spent his days lurking in the pool there, in the shape of a salmon. He was there for months, waiting for the gods.

One morning as he sat by the fire in his house, Loki started to wonder how the gods might try to catch him if they knew he was hiding as a salmon in Glinting's Pool. He thought about Aegir and his wife Ran, and about Ran's net. If Ran could throw a net above the sea to catch ships, then it would be easy to drop a net into the water and take out a fish. As he thought about this, Loki picked up some linen twine, and he started to tie it into a mesh, just as fishing nets have been made ever since.

Then he heard the voices of the gods coming along the valley. He jumped up and, throwing his net onto the fire, he ran outside to Glinting's Pool, where he dived into the water in the shape of a salmon.

When the gods reached Loki's house, they went inside and looked around. The first to go in was the wisest of all. His name was Kvasir, and he could see what is hidden from other people.

When Kvasir saw the fire he said, 'Loki was here just now. There's still heat in the fire.'

But when he looked into the ashes and saw the shape where the net had burned he said, 'Loki has made himself a mesh of strings to catch fish, and he has burnt it on the fire. It's my belief that we must look for Loki in the water, and he will be in the shape of a salmon.'

Kvasir showed the gods how to make a net, just like the one they saw in the ashes which Loki had made. When it was ready, they went to Glinting's Pool and lowered the net into the water. Thor took one end of the net, and the rest of the gods stood on the other side of the pool with the other end.

They dragged the net through the water, but Loki swam down to the bottom of the pool and hid between two big stones. When the gods dragged the net over the stones, Heimdal saw something moving deep in the water but they couldn't catch it. They pulled the net out again and weighted the bottom with stones, so that nothing could get underneath.

Then they dropped their net in the water again. This time, as they were dragging it through the pool, a salmon swam up through the water and away in front of the net down the river. They dragged the net all along the river to the sea, and the salmon swam ahead of them.

But when he reached the end of the river where it flowed out into the sea, the salmon turned back and swam up against the net. Then he leaped right out of the water over the top of the net, and he dashed back up the river to Glinting's Pool.

The gods took the net back up to the waterfall to drag the river again. But this time, Thor waded down the middle of the river, while the others went ahead with the net stretched between them.

Slowly, the gods made their way downriver, and the salmon swam in front of them. When they drew near the sea and he tasted salt water once more, Loki saw that there were just two ways open to him, either to end his life in the salt sea, or to take a chance by jumping the net again. He turned and jumped high over the net, but Thor reached out and grabbed him in mid-air.

Loki slithered through Thor's fingers, until Thor was holding him just above the tail, but then he gripped so hard that he squeezed the fish out of shape, so that salmon are pinched in tight above the tail even to this day.

The gods took Loki back to his cave.

They set three stone slabs on edge in the cave, with a hole in each stone. They caught his sons Vali and Nari, and they changed Vali into a wolf so that he tore his brother Nari apart. They unwound Nari's guts and used them as ropes to tie Loki onto the stones. One stone was under his shoulders, one was under his hips, and the third under his knees. Then these ropes turned to iron.

Skadi used the sinews of the wolf to tie a snake above him, so that its head was above Loki's head, and the venom from the snake's mouth dripped into Loki's face.

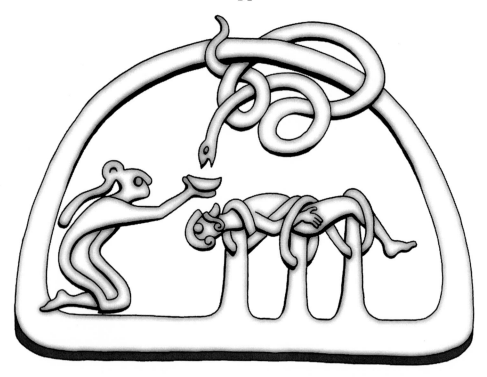

That is how they left him, and that is the torture the gods decided Loki should suffer for what he had done until the end of the earth.

Loki's wife Sigyn went to find him there, and she holds a bowl above him to catch the dripping venom. Slowly the drips fill Sigyn's bowl, until she has to go outside to empty it. While she's gone, the venom drips again in Loki's face. Then he writhes and struggles so fiercely that the whole earth shakes, and that is what people call an 'earthquake'.

That is where Loki is lying now, tied to those stones in the cave. And there he will lie until the Doom of the Powers.

Kvasir's Blood

Kvasir was the wisest man who has ever lived. All Father shaped him long ago from the spittle of all the gods, both Aesir and Vanir, when they came together to make peace. And as he was shaped from their spittle, so Kvasir had the wisdom of all the gods.

Since that time, Kvasir had gone far and wide throughout the world, sharing his wisdom wherever he went. No one could ask him a question that he couldn't answer, and it was Kvasir who had taught the gods how to trap Loki in a net.

There were two dwarfs called Fialar and Galar, who lived in a cave on a steep cliff overlooking a firth where the sea came in among the mountains. They heard of Kvasir and his wisdom, and of how everyone liked him to visit.

'Who is he that everyone likes him?' they asked each other. 'What's so great about this Kvasir? Who does he think he is?'

So when Kvasir came to visit them, they led him to a dark chamber deep inside their cave. There they strung him up and slit his throat, and they drained his blood into two pots and a barrel. That barrel is called Soul Stirrer, and the pots are called Jar and Offering. They mixed his blood with honey and made it into mead.

'Now we have the wisdom of Kvasir all to ourselves,' they said. But they told everyone that Kvasir had been so wise that he had choked on his own knowledge, because there was no one clever enough to ask him questions.

Not long after this, an etin called Billing came with his wife to see the dwarfs. They took Billing out in their fishing boat on the firth, but his wife stayed on shore. It was high tide, but there were rocks hidden in the water where a boat could easily be wrecked.

The dwarfs took their boat into rough water, where the waves went over a rocky skerry that was covered by the tide. The boat overturned in the waves, and Billing sank straight to the bottom and drowned. But the dwarfs got their boat upright again, and rowed back to shore.

When they told his wife that Billing had drowned, she started to weep and wail loudly.

Fialar asked her, 'Would it ease your heart if you could look out across the water, and see the place where Billing drowned?'

She said that she'd like to see that, so Fialar pointed out through the cave mouth to where the sea grew choppy as it went over the skerry, and she went out to look. Then he said to Galar, 'Go up on the roof above the doorway, and drop a millstone on her head, will you? I've had quite enough of her howling.'

So Galar dropped the millstone on her and flattened her. Then it was quiet again.

The etin Billing and his wife had three children. Their sons were called Suttung and Baugi, and their daughter was called Rinda. When his parents didn't come back from Fialar's cave, Suttung went to see the dwarfs himself.

'You'll pay with your lives for the death of my father,' he said, 'and for my mother's life.'

The dwarfs said, 'You could leave here laden with riches in gold and in silver, if you will agree to spare our lives.'

'No riches can pay for the life of my mother, or for my father's death,' said Suttung. He picked up the dwarfs and waded out into the firth until he reached the rocky skerry that could now be seen above the waves.

'The tide is low,' said Suttung, 'but when it rises, the waves will wash you off this rock and drown you in the sea.'

Then Fialar said, 'There are two pots of mead, hidden deep in our cave. Nothing is more precious among gods or men. It was made from the blood of Kvasir the Wise, and in that mead is the wisdom of all the gods. That wisdom will be yours, if you spare our lives.'

Then Suttung took them back to their cave, and they showed him the two pots, Jar and Offering, filled with the mead. But Suttung saw the barrel Soul Stirrer, and he took that from them too.

When they saw him take the barrel, the dwarfs cursed Suttung saying, 'You shall never keep that mead in peace. It will bring you only worry and care, and it will be stolen from you, just as you have stolen it from us.'

'No burden is better than a barrelful of wisdom,' said Suttung. Then he strapped the barrel to his back, and set off for home with a pot in each hand.

Suttung wanted to be sure the mead was safe, so he didn't taste even a single drop. He set his daughter Gunnlod to guard it, and he told her never to take a sip. Then he buried her with the mead under the mountain of Knit Crags. That mountain stands near Suttung's farm, and he would watch the smoke as it rose from Gunnlod's fire deep inside the mountain.

But All Father had been watching from his high seat of Lid Shelf, from where he can see across all worlds. He had seen Suttung walking home with the mead on his back, and he knew then what had really happened to Kvasir and his wisdom.

He also knew that he had to win back Kvasir's wisdom for the gods.

Bale Work

Odin put on his hooded cowl, and he took the name of 'Bale Work', which means 'worker of hay bales' or 'worker of evils'. He set off barefoot into Etinhome, until he came to a meadow where nine men were working.

They were mowing the hay, cutting the tall grass with their long scythes. Odin asked them, 'Would you like to sit and rest, while I sharpen your scythes?'

They said they would, so he took a whetstone from his belt and sharpened the scythes. When the men set to with their scythes again, the work seemed much easier than before, and they said, 'Our scythes cut much better now. Can we buy the whetstone from you?'

'You can't all have it,' said Odin, 'but I'll sell it gladly to any one of you who will give me a fair price for it.'

Then they all started to argue about who should buy the stone. 'Sell it to me!' said one. 'No, sell it to me!' said another. 'You can't have it. I want it,' said a third.

Odin threw the whetstone up into the air, and they all ran to catch it. They started to fight over it, and with their sharp scythes they cut each others' throats. It wasn't long before all those men were lying dead around the stone.

Odin picked up his whetstone and went on his way.

He asked to stay that night at the house of the etin Baugi, Billing's son. Next morning he asked the farmer, 'Why do you look so sad and worried? Would it ease your heart if you could share your sorrows?'

'Yesterday, I had nine farmhands,' said Baugi. 'Today, they all lie dead in the meadow with the hay uncut around them. I don't know where I'll get more workers now.'

'My name is Bale Work,' said Odin, 'and I can do the work of nine farmhands for you.'

'If you can do nine men's work,' said Baugi, 'what wages would you want?'

'All I'd ask would be a swig of the mead that your brother Suttung has,' said Bale Work, 'which the dwarfs paid him for Billing's death.'

'That mead isn't mine to give,' said Baugi, 'and Suttung keeps it all for himself.'

'But Billing was your father too, so you should have a share of the mead, and I can help you get it.'

'That's true,' said Baugi. 'If you work for me all summer long and do the work well, then I'll gladly go with you to ask for the mead.'

So Bale Work stayed on Baugi's farm all through the summer, and he did the work of nine men. He cut the hay for Baugi's cattle. He cut the corn for Baugi's bread. He cut the reeds to thatch Baugi's roof. He worked from dawn until dusk, and he made his bed wherever he worked.

One morning, Baugi's sister Rinda found him among the reeds. 'It's a shame to see such a fine man forced to sleep in the reeds,' she said. 'Come to my bower this evening, and you shall sleep in my bed.'

But when Bale Work went to her bower that night, the dogs began to bark and Baugi's warriors rushed out with swords and spears. Then Bale Work slipped back into the shadows and went away.

The next day, Rinda came to see Bale Work and she gave him a kiss. 'Come back at midnight,' she said. 'My dogs will be tied up, and Baugi's men will be sleeping.'

So Bale Work went back to Rinda's bower when the house was asleep. He opened the door, and he crept inside. Rinda lay sleeping there, but he couldn't wake her. Her dogs were tied to the end of the bed, and they snarled and strained to bite at him. He went away again, but he remembered the words of Mimir, that it was Rinda's son who would take vengeance for Balder.

The next day when Rinda came to see Bale Work, he split a twig into two halves and wrote on them in runes with his knife. Then he gave one half to Rinda.

'Take this, and put it under your pillow,' he said.

But when she lay down on her bed, her belly swelled and she called out that she was going to give birth, and she cried out with the pangs of labour.

Baugi asked Bale Work what to do.

'I know a midwife called Witch who can help her,' said Bale Work.

Baugi told him to fetch the midwife, so Bale Work went off. Then he dressed himself in woman's clothes like a witch, and he came back to see Rinda. Now, there was no one to stop him getting close to her, and he stayed with her all through the day and through the night.

In the morning, Rinda gave birth to a son, and she called him Vali. Then the midwife left her.

Vali grew up very fast. When he was just one night old he said goodbye to his mother, and he took a sword to look for Balder's killer. He neither washed his face nor combed his hair, before he had killed Hoder and burned his body on a funeral pyre.

On the first day of winter Bale Work asked Baugi for his wages, and they both set off to see Suttung to ask about the mead.

Suttung greeted them saying, 'Brother Baugi, you are welcome here. But why have you brought your farmhand with you?'

Baugi said, 'Bale Work has done the work of nine men on my farm this summer, and I have had no other help. As payment, he asks for a swig of your mead.'

Suttung looked at them hard and said, 'That mead was bought with our own father's life. I have set the mead under Knit Crags, with my own daughter Gunnlod to guard it. No one will ever taste it!'

So Baugi and Bale Work left the hall empty handed.

Bale Work said, 'We'll have to try another way to get the mead.'

'That's a good idea,' said Baugi.

They went up onto the mountainside of Knit Crags, and Bale Work took out a little auger.

'Bore a hole with this,' he said, 'if it will go through.'

Baugi started boring into the mountain with the auger. He worked for some time and as he dug deeper into the cliff, the auger grew longer so he could bore deep into the mountain. After a while Baugi stopped and took the auger out.

'There, that goes right through,' he said.

Bale Work went up to the hole and he blew into it, but the dust came back in his face so he knew that the hole didn't go all the way through.

'It looks as if you're trying to trick me,' he said. 'Go deeper this time.'

Baugi started work again, and bored deeper into the mountain. When he had finished, Bale Work went up to the hole, and this time he blew the dust through to the heart of the mountain. Then he knew that the hole went right through.

Bale Work turned himself into a little snake, and slithered through the hole. Baugi tried to stab at him with the auger, but Bale Work was too quick for him and he crawled through to the cavern on the other side.

The hall inside the mountain was decked with splendid tapestries, and Gunnlod sat in a gilded high seat in front of the fire. But for all her finery, she had not seen a friendly face since her father had walled her up under the mountain at the start of the summer.

When Bale Work dropped to the floor he took the shape of a handsome man, and Gunnlod greeted him happily. He stayed three nights with her, and she let him take three drinks of mead.

On the first night, he drained the pot called Jar.

The next night he drained Offering.

On the third night, he drained the barrel which was called Soul Stirrer, and then he had all the mead.

Odin turned himself into an eagle and flew up through the smoke hole in the roof of the cave, out through the top of the mountain and away home towards Asgarth.

But Suttung had been keeping watch over Knit Crags and when he saw the eagle fly from the mountaintop, he took on his own eagle shape and set off after him.

Odin flew as hard as he could towards Asgarth. He had set off first but he had drunk heavily, and no burden is worse than a bellyful of drink. So Suttung flew faster, and he soon began to gain on him.

When Odin saw Asgarth's Wall ahead of him, he could see behind him the spread of Suttung's tail feathers and the curve of his talons. And before Odin flew over the Wall, he felt the draft of Suttung's wingbeats, as those talons reached out towards him.

But once Odin had cleared the Wall, Suttung looked down and saw all the gods gathered there with their spears and bows, so he turned round and flew for home.

When the gods saw Odin flying back, they put out all Asgarth's pots and kettles below the Wall. Odin opened his mouth and spewed the mead out into the pots.

That mead was made from the blood of Kvasir, and Kvasir had the wisdom of all the gods because he was made from the spittle of the gods. So now in that mead there is the wisdom of all the gods.

The next day, the frost etins came to Asgarth and wanted to see Odin.

'Where is Bale Work?' they asked. 'Is he with the gods? He has taken our mead from us, and we want it back.'

All Father said, 'We have never met this man called Bale Work, but if he comes here to see us then I promise to take your mead from him.'

When the etins had gone, Odin shared out the mead. Some of it he gave to the gods, and some of it he drank himself. But some he kept and he gives it to those people who are skilled in making poems. The greatest of poets are those who have drunk most deeply of Kvasir's blood, and the finest of poetry is composed from the purest draught of Odin's mead.

But when Odin was flying home to Asgarth, when he felt the wingbeats of Suttung coming behind him and could almost feel the claws in his back, he was so scared that he wet himself. So some of the mead fell in the mud outside the Asgarth's Wall, and it is there for anyone to take. But a draught of that will lead only to meaningless drivel and the worst of doggerel.

The Doom of the Powers

These are the things that have been. The gods rule now in Asgarth as they have since the beginning. Loki lies bound below the mountain. The wolf Fenrir is bound on the island. People are born; people die. Some go down to Shadow Home, and some join the gods in Asgarth.

But nothing is for ever.

The time will come when Fenrir and Loki will break free. The etins will storm across Midgarth, while the fiery sons of Muspell ride over the Rainbow Bridge. The gods will set out from Asgarth against them, and the battle that is fought between them then will be the last that is fought in the age of this world.

Before that time comes, there will be three hard winters, when there will be fighting throughout the world. People will kill each other for greed and gold, and brothers will show no mercy.

Then the earth will suffer the Awful Winter, when the snows will drift everywhere, there will be hard frosts and bitter winds, and the Sun will do no good. This winter will last for the length of three winters with no summer between, until the wolf Scorn that follows the Sun will catch it and swallow it. And Moongarm will catch up with the Moon, and the stars will flee from the sky.

In Gallows Wood, the fair red cockerel Fialar will crow so loud that all Etinhome will hear him. Then Golden Comb will crow to the gods, the cockerel that wakes the Lone Warriors in Kill Hall. And under the earth, his cry is answered by the rust red cockerel at the Gates of Hel.

The whole earth and all the hills and mountains will tremble and shake, so that trees are uprooted where they stand, and all the chains and tethers will break.

Cliffs will crumble and troll women topple. The dwarfs will moan beside their doors of stone. The dead will tread the road from Hel. The World Tree will shudder and its boughs will shake, and there will be nothing in heaven or on earth that is not afraid.

Then the leash Gleipnir will break, and Fenrir will be free. The wolf's jaws will gape so wide that his top jaw touches the sky and his bottom jaw scrapes the ground, and fire shoots out from his eyes and his nostrils.

The seas will flood across the earth, as the Great Monster rises in anger from the deeps, and comes up on land spewing poison that spurts over sea and sky.

Then etins will rush out from Etinhome.

The etin Frost will sail out from Sleet Waves on the ship Nail Farer, and all the frost etins with him. That ship is made from dead people's fingernails. Loki steers the ship, and it is swept along on the flood as the World Snake writhes and drives over the waves.

Then the sky breaks open, and all the sons of Muspell ride through. The etin Surt leads them from the south in a blaze of flame, and his sword will shine brighter than the Sun. And when they ride over Bifrost, the Rainbow Bridge will crack beneath their weight. Fire leaps up to the highest heaven, but they will ride on until they come to the battlefield of War Surge.

Heimdal sets Yeller Horn to his lips, which has never once been blown before. That horn blast will ring out across all Asgarth to summon the gods. Then All Father will ride to Mimir's Well, to ask his counsel. The gods will meet once more on Ida Field, before they set out to the slaughter.

The Lone Warriors will stream out through Kill Hall's five hundred and forty doors in ranks eight hundred wide, to do battle against the etins. They will meet on the battlefield of War Surge. That battlefield is a hundred miles wide and another hundred miles long.

Odin rides out in front on Slider, with his golden helm on his head and his spear Flincher in his hand. Storm Rider will stand beside him, with his mighty hammer Miller held in his iron gloves, and his belt around his waist.

Odin will ride against Fenrir, but he falls between the wolf's gaping jaws. Thor will not be able to help him, because he must fight the Great Monster. But Odin's son Vidar steps up and strikes with his foot in Fenrir's jaws. The sole of Vidar's shoe is made from the leather left over from all the shoes that have ever been made, and it's very thick. He puts his foot in Fenrir's mouth, and tears the wolf open with his hands.

That is Vidar's revenge for his father's death.

Hel's dog Garm will break free and will fight against Tyr. It is a very vicious animal, and they will both be killed there.

Loki will do battle with Heimdal, and there they will kill each other.

Frey will go to battle without his sword, but he fights hard and long against Surt with a stag's antler. Surt's sword is forged from burning flame, and he strikes Frey with that blade so Frey falls there too. Then Surt will fling his fire over all the earth, so that everything is burned in the flames.

Thor strides out against the Great Monster, to do battle for a second time. He'll raise his hammer and strike the serpent dead, and no question about it this time! But a cloud of poison will rise from the serpent, so Thor can take only nine steps away from there before the poison overwhelms him, and he too falls dead.

The greatest of gods and etins will fall there. Everything will be lost. Heaven and earth will be burned. The gods, the Lone Warriors and all mankind will be dead. The whole of the earth will lie under the seas. Only Gimle in highest heaven will not be harmed, and the hall of Brimir which stands there.

But Life and Life Striver, a man and a woman, will find shelter amongst the branches of Mimir's Wood. There they will stay unharmed by Surt's fire, and their food will be the morning dew.

The earth will rise anew from the waters, and it will be green and beautiful. Crops will grow in the fields without being sown. The eagle will fly from the sunlit crags to catch fish in the clear water.

Life and Life Striver will leave the shelter of Mimir's Wood, and go down onto the new earth. From their children and their children's children, there will come a race of people who will live over the whole of the earth.

New gods will come to Ida Field. Vidar and Vali will be there. Thor's sons, Magni and Modi, Strength and Bravery, will come bringing with them the hammer Miller. Balder will come back from Shadow Home to rule among the gods, and beside him will sit his brother Hoder and his wife Nanna.

They will come back to Ida Field, and there in the grass they will find the golden chessmen that the Aesir had owned. They will talk and tell stories about what happened in days gone by, about Fenrir and the Great Monster, about Thor and Odin, Sif and Frigg, about Frey and Freya, and all the gods of old.

Index of Names

Aegir (*Ægir*) : an etin, ruler of the sea; 119-21, 130, 157-9, 165.

All Father (*Alfǫðr*) : see '**Odin**'

All Swift, see '**Early Waker & All Swift**'

Asgarth (*Ásgarðr*) : the home of the gods; 31, 32, 37-42, 45, 47, 48, 49, 54, 61-7, 70-1, 77-8, 80, 87, 91, 92-7, 119, 132-4, 142, 153, 155, 156, 158, 181-3, 184, 187.

Ash & Elm (*Askr, Embla*) : the first people; 44.

Audhumla (*Auðhumla, Auðumbla*) : the first cow, her licking revealed the first of the gods; 27.

Aurboda (*Aurboða*) : the mother of Gerd; 54.

Aurvandil (*Aurvandill*) : a man, his wife is Groa; 138-9.

Balder (*Baldr*) : a god, he is killed by his brother Hoder; 39, 67-8, 147-56, 158, 161, 178-9, 191.

Bale Work (*Bǫlverkr*) : a name taken by Odin, 175-181, 183; see also '**Odin**'

Barrey (*Barrey, Barri*) : the island where Gerd agrees to meet Frey, sometimes identified with Barra in the Western Isles; 57-8.

Baugi (*Baugi*) : the etin Suttung's brother; 172, 176-80.

Bee Leg (*Býleiptr, Býleistr*) : an etin, Loki's brother; 41.

Being, Becoming & Necessity (*Urðr, Verðandi, Skuld*) : the three Norns; 32-4.

Bergelmir (*Bergelmir*) : an etin, he escaped in a boat from the blood of Ymir which drowned the other etins; 28.

Bestla (*Bestla*) : mother of Odin, Vili and Ve; daughter of the etin Bolthor; 27, see '**Introduction**' 17.

Bifrost (*Bifrǫst, Bilrǫst*) : the Rainbow; 29, 40, 52, 63, 184, 186.

Billing (*Billingr, Gillingr*) : father of Suttung, Baugi and Rinda, he is killed by the dwarfs Fialar and Galar; 153, 171-2, 176-7, see 'Introduction' 19.

Black Elfhome (*Svartálfaheimr*) : home of the dwarfs, Ivaldi's sons; 41, 77-8.

Blast Home (*Þrymheimr*) : home of the etin Thiassi and his daughter Skadi; 64, 66, 69.

Blind (*Blindi, Blindr*) : see '**Odin**'

Bloody Hoof (*Blóðughófi*) : Frey's horse, which he gives to Skirnir; 56.

Boat Town (*Nóatún*) : home of Niord; 50, 68-9.

Bolthor (*Bǫlþor, Bǫlþorn*) : an etin, Bestla's father (Bestla is Odin's mother); 17, see 'Introduction' 17.

Bor (*Borr, Burr*) : Buri's son, the father of Odin, Vili and Ve; 27-8.

Bragi (*Bragi*) : a god, his wife is the goddess Idun; 62-5, 159-60.

Bright Home (*Glaðsheimr*) : the meeting house of the gods; 40-1, 92, 97, 119.

Bright Secret (*Heiðrún*) : a goat, her milk is the mead of Kill Hall; 38.

Brimir (*Brimir*) : probably an etin, his hall is said to be in Gimle; in *Vǫluspá* st.9 he seems to be identical with Ymir; 189.

Brising Necklace (*Brísingamen*) : Freya's necklace; 51-3, 76, 87-8.

Broad Gleam (*Breiðablik*) : Balder's hall; 39, 147.

Brokk & Sindri (*Brokkr, Sindri*) : the dwarfs who forge Thor's Hammer; in some versions Sindri is called Eitri; 78-84, 152.

Buri (*Búri*) : the first god, the father of Bor; 27.

Cloud Legs (*Mǫkkurkálfi*) : Hrungnir's earthen helper in his fight with Thor; 135, 137.

Corpse Sands (*Nástrǫnd*) : the place where Hel has her hall of Sleet Fall; 71, 154.

Dizziness (*Vimur*) : a river in Etinhome; Thor crosses it on his way to Geirrod's Garth; 143.

Doom of the Powers (*Ragnarǫk, Ragnarøkr*) : the last battle; 37, 40, 75, 128, 169, 184-91

Dripper (*Draupnir*) : Odin's gold armring made by the dwarf Brokk; 82, 94, 152, 155.

Dromi (*Drómi*) : the second leash made for Fenrir; 72-4.

Dvalin, Alfrik, Berling & Grer (*Dvalinn, Álfrigg, Berlingr, Grérr*) : the dwarfs who make the Brising Necklace; 51.

Early Waker & All Swift (*Árvakr, Alsviðr*) : the horses which pull the Sun through the sky; 29.

Egil (*Egill*) : the father of Thialfi and Roeskva; 99-102.

Eldir, see '**Fimafeng & Eldir**'

Elfhome (*Álfheimr*) : Frey's home in Asgarth; 54.

Elli (*Elli*) : 'Old Age', Thor's wrestling opponent in Outgarth; 115, 117.

Elm, see '**Ash & Elm**'

Etinhome (*Jǫtunheimr*) : the home of the etins; 30, 31, 35, 41-2, 54, 56, 59, 64, 66, 70, 86-9, 92, 94-5, 97, 99, 102, 118, 120-2, 130, 131, 133-4, 138, 141-3, 153, 158, 175.

Famine (*Sultr*) : Hel's knife; 71, 155.

Fenrir (*Fenrir, Fenrisúlfr*) : a wolf, Loki's son; 71-4, 158, 162, 184-5, 188, 191.

Fialar & Galar (*Fjalarr, Galarr*) : the dwarfs who kill Kvasir and Billing; 170-3.

Fialar (*Fjalarr*) : a cockerel in Etinhome; 185.

Fimafeng & Eldir (*Fimafengr, Eldir*) : Aegir's servants; 158-9.

Fire Sooty, see '**Sea Sooty, Fire Sooty & On Sooty**'

Flincher (*Gugnir, Gungnir*) : Odin's spear; 82, 188.

Folk Field (*Fólkvangr*) : Freya's realm in Asgarth; 50.

Forseti (*Forseti*) : Balder's son; 147.

Frey (*Freyr*) : a god, the son of Niord; 48, 50, 54-8, 73, 81-3, 151, 158, 162, 189, 191.

Freya (*Freyja*) : a goddess, the daughter of Niord; 48, 50-4, 64, 76, 85, 87-91, 92, 94-5, 97, 133-4, 140, 151, 158, 161, 191.

Frigg (*Frigg*) : a goddess, the wife of Odin, she is the queen of the Aesir; 39, 148-9, 151-3, 155-6, 158, 161, 191.

Frost (*Frostr*) : leader of the Frost etins; 186.

Fulla (*Fulla*) : Frigg's maidservant; 39, 155.

Galar, see 'Fialar & Galar'

Garm (*Garmr*) : a monstrous dog or hound; 188.

Geirrod (*Geirrøðr*) : an etin; his daughters are Yelp and Grip; 140-6.

Geirrod's Garth (*Geirrøðargarðar*) : 140, 143-4.

Gerd (*Gerðr*) : Gymir's daughter, she marries Frey; 54-8.

Gimle (*Gimlé*) : a region in highest heaven, home of the righteous dead; 189.

Ginnunga Gap (*Ginnungagap*) : the primordial void; 25, 28.

Gleipnir (*Gleipnir*) : the third leash which finally binds Fenrir; 73-5, 186.

Glinting (*Fránangr, Fránangrs Forsi*) : the waterfall where Loki hides as a salmon; 164-6.

Gna (*Gná*) : Frigg's messenger, she rides the horse Hoof Thrower; 39, 156.

Gold Mane (*Gullfaxi*) : Hrungnir's horse; Thor gives it to his son Magni; 131, 134, 138.

Gold Tuft (*Gulltoppr*) : Heimdall's horse; 151.

Goldbright (*Gullveig*) : a goddess of the Vanir; her treatment by the Aesir leads to war between the gods; 45-7.

Golden Bristle (*Gullinbursti*) : Frey's boar, forged by Sindri and Brokk; 82, 151.

Golden Comb (*Gullinkambi*) : a cockerel in Asgarth; 185.

Great Monster (*Jǫrmungandr*) : a serpent, Loki's son; 70-1, 117, 120, 125-8, 186, 188-9, 191.

Greed & Hunger (*Freki, Geri*) : Odin's wolves; 38.

Greybeard (*Hárbarðr*) : see 'Odin'

Grid (*Gríðr*) : an etin woman, mother of Vidar; 142-5.

Grip, see 'Yelp & Grip'

Gritgarth (*Grjótúnagarðar*) : home of the etin Hrungnir; 131, 134-6.

Groa (*Gróa*): a witch or healer, her spells loosen the whetstone in Thor's forehead; 138-9.

Gunnlod (*Gunnlǫð*): daughter of the etin Suttung, she guards the mead Kvasir's Blood; 174, 179-81.

Gymir (*Gymir*): an etin, father of Gerd; 54, 56.

Hardbeater (*Fárbauti*): an etin, father of Loki; 41.

Hate (*Hati*): the wolf that chases the moon; 30.

Heath (*Lyngvi*): the island where Fenrir is bound; 73.

Heaven Cliff (*Himinbjǫrg*): Heimdal's hall; 40.

Heimdal (*Heimdalr, Heimdallr, Heimdali*): a god, he keeps watch from the top of Bifrost; 40, 42-3, 52-3, 63, 88, 95, 151, 166, 187-8.

Hel (*Hel*): ruler of Shadow Home, Loki's daughter; 71, 151-6, 163, 185, 188.

Hel Blind (*Helblindi*): an etin, Loki's brother; 41.

Hermod (*Hermóðr*): Balder's brother, he rides on Slider to visit Balder in Shadow Home; 147, 153-6.

Hlin (*Hlín*): see 'Frigg'

Hoder (*Hǫðr*): a god, Balder's blind brother and killer; 147, 149-50, 179, 191.

Hoenir (*Hœnir*): a god, he is given to the Vanir but they send him back; 44, 48-9, 59, 61.

Hooded (*Grímnir, Síðhǫttr*): see 'Odin'

Hoof Thrower (*Hófvarpnir*): Gna's horse; 39.

Hope (*Ván*): the river which runs from Fenrir's mouth; 75.

Horror (*Yggr*): see 'Odin'

Hroth (*Hroðr*): an etin woman, mother of Tyr; 122, 129.

Hrungnir (*Hrungnir*): an etin; 131-7.

Hugi (*Hugi*): 'Thought', Thialfi's competitor in Outgarth; 110-1, 117.

Hunger (*Hungr*): Hel's plate; 71, 155; for Odin's wolf **Hunger**, see 'Greed & Hunger'

Hymir (*Hymir*): an etin, father of Tyr; 121-9, 131, 157.

Ida Field (*Iðavǫllr*) : the meeting place in Asgarth where Bright Home stands; 40, 43, 47, 81, 148, 187, 191.

Idun (*Iðunn*) : a goddess, she keeps the Apples of Life for the Aesir; 61-6, 158, 160-1, see 'Introduction' 19.

Ill Boding (*Angrboða*) : Loki's etin wife, mother of Fenrir, Hel and the Great Monster; 70.

Ironknife (*Járnsaxa*) : an etin woman, the mother of Thor's sons Magni and Modi; 138.

Ironwood (*Járnviðr*) : a forest in Etinhome; 30.

Ivaldi (*Ívaldi*) : father of the dwarfs who make Sif's hair (possibly also father of Idun and Thiassi); 77-8, see 'Introduction' 19.

Jar (*Boðn*) : one of the three vessels in which the mead Kvasir's Blood is kept; 171, 173, 181.

Jewel & Treasure (*Hnoss, Gersimi*) : Freya's daughters; 50.

Kill Choosers (*Valkyrjar*) : magical women who choose the Lone Warriors; 37, 151.

Kill Hall (*Valhǫll*) : Odin's hall, where the Lone Warriors feast; 37, 132-3, 149, 185, 187.

Knit Crags (*Hnitbjǫrg*) : the mountain where Suttung stores the mead; 174, 179-80.

Kvasir (*Kvasir*) : the wisest of men, made by Odin from the spittle of the gods; 47-8, 163, 165, 170-1, 173-4, 182-3.

Leafy or **Needle** (*Laufey, Nál*) : Loki's mother; 41-2, 156.

Leeward Isle (*Hlésey*) : home of the sea etin Aegir; often identified with the Danish island of Læsø; 157, 159.

Leyding (*Lœðingr*) : the first leash with which the gods try to bind Fenrir; 72-4.

Lid Shelf (*Hliðskjálf*) : Odin's high seat, from which he can look over all the upper worlds; 40-1, 45, 54, 133, 174.

Life & Life Striver (*Líf, Lífþrasir*) : the two people who will survive the destruction of the world; 190.

Logi (*Logi*) : 'Flame', Loki's opponent in Outgarth; his brothers are Aegir who rules the sea and Kari who rules the winds; 110, 117, 120.

Loki (*Loki*) : a god, the son of Leafy and Hardbeater; 41-3, 44-5, 52-3, 59, 61-6, 69, 70-1, 76-8, 82-4, 85-91, 93, 95-8, 99-100, 102-4, 107, 109-10, 117-8, 141-3, 148-51, 156, 158-63, 164-9, 170, 184, 186, 188.

Lone Warriors (*Einherjar*) : the fallen warriors in Odin's hall, they train for battle in readiness for the Doom of the Powers; 37-8, 40, 133, 185, 187, 189.

Magni & Modi (*Magni, Móði*) : Thor's sons, 'Strength' and 'Courage'; 138, 191.

Memory, see '**Thought & Memory**'

Midgarth (*Miðgarðr*) : the world of people, or the wall which defends it from the world of Etinhome; 31-2, 34, 45, 62-3, 92, 122, 184.

Miller (*Mjǫllnir*) : Thor's hammer; 80, 82-3, 85-8, 90-1, 92, 97, 101-3, 105-7, 118, 127-30, 134, 136-7, 142, 162-3, 188, 191.

Mimir (*Mímir, Mímr*) : an etin who guards the Well of Wisdom, also a god killed by the Vanir whose head is preserved by Odin - possibly two separate figures both representing wisdom; 35-6, 48-9, 70-1, 153, 178, see 'Introduction' 17.

Mimir's Wood (*Mímameiðr, Hodd-Mímis holt, Yggdrasil*) : a tree which exists in all the Nine Worlds; 31-6, 57, 62, 190.

Mirkwood (*Myrkviðr*) : a legendary forest, the place where Thiassi abducts Idun is described by Snorri simply as 'in a certain wood' (*í skóg nǫkkurn*); 62-3.

Modgud (*Móðguðr*) : an etin woman at Yell's Bridge; 154.

Modi, see '**Magni & Modi**'

Moon, see '**Sun & Moon**'

Moongarm (*Mánagarmr*) : a wolf in Etinhome, that will swallow the Sun, Moon and Stars; 30, 185.

Muspell (*Múspell*) : the primordial world of fire; 25-6, 29, 40, 162, 184, 186.

Nail Farer (*Naglfar, Naglfari*) : a ship; 186.

Nanna (*Nanna*) : a goddess, Balder's wife; 39, 147, 151, 155, 191.

Nari & Vali (*Nari* or *Narfi, Váli*) : Loki's sons with Sigyn; 70, 168.

Nine Worlds (*Níu Heimar*) : the whole of existence, being Asgarth, Midgarth and Etinhome along with their respective heavens and underworlds; 31, 37-9, 43, 77, 142, 156.

Niord (*Njǫrðr*) : a god of the Vanir, he marries the etin Skadi; 48, 50, 54-5, 68-9, 158.

Norns (*Nornir*) : see '**Being, Becoming and Necessity**'

North, South, East & West (*Norðri, Suðri, Austri, Vestri*) : the dwarfs who hold up the heavens; 28.

Odin (*Óðinn*) : a god, leader of the Aesir, known as All Father; 27, 31-6, 37-43, 44-5, 47-9, 54, 57, 59-61, 66-7, 69, 70-1, 73, 81-3, 88, 93-5, 98, 119-21, 131-4, 138, 142, 147, 151-5, 158-9, 161, 170, 174, 175-83, 187-8, 191.

Offering (*Són*) ; one of the three vessels in which the mead Kvasir's Blood is kept; 171, 173, 181.

On Sooty, see '**Sea Sooty, Fire Sooty & On Sooty**'

Oth (*Óðr*) : a god, Freya's husband; 50.

Outgarth (*Útgarðr*) : a stronghold in Etinhome; 99, 102, 107-8, 109-18, 119-21.

Outgarth Loki (*Útgarða-Loki*) : king of Outgarth, possibly another incarnation of Loki himself; 99, 107, 109-18.

Ran (*Rán*) : the etin Aegir's wife, she drowns sailors in her net; 157-8, 165.

Rattletusk (*Ratatǫskr*) : the squirrel in the branches of Mimir's Wood; 32, 34.

Rinda (*Rindr*) : Billing's daughter, mother of Vali; 153, 172, 177-8, see 'Introduction' 19.

Ring Horn (*Hringhorni*) : Balder's ship; 151.

Roeskva, see '**Thialfi & Roeskva**'

Scorn (*Skǫll, Skoll*) : the wolf that chases the sun; 30, 185.

Sea Sooty, Fire Sooty & On Sooty (*Sæhrímnir, Eldhrímnir, Andhrímnir*) : the pig served every night in Kill Hall, the pot it is cooked in and the cook who cooks it; 38.

Seat Roomy (*Sessrúmnir*) : Freya's hall; 50.

Seether (*Hvergelmir*) : a well in Shadow Home, home of Spite Cutter; 34.

Shadow Home (*Niflheim, Niflheimr*) : the Viking underworld (literally 'Mist Home'); 34, 71, 97, 151-6, 163, 184, 191.

Sick Bed (*Kǫr*) : Hel's bed; 71.

Sif (*Sif*) : a goddess, Thor's wife, Loki cuts off her hair; 39, 76-7, 81, 83, 133, 158, 162, 191.

Sigyn (*Sigyn*) : a goddess, Loki's wife; 70, 169.

Sindri, see '**Brokk & Sindri**'

Singing Stone (*Singasteinn*) : a rock in the sea, Loki and Heimdal fight there as seals; 52.

Skadi (*Skaði*) : the etin Thiassi's daughter, she marries Niord; 66-9, 158, 168.

Ski Blader (*Skíðblaðnir*) : Frey's ship; 82.

Skirnir (*Skírnir*) : Frey's servant and companion; 55-8, 73.

Skrymir (*Skrýmir*) : a name taken by Outgarth-Loki, 104-8, 116, 163; see also '**Outgarth-Loki**'

Sleet Fall (*Éljúðnir*) : Hel's hall; 71, 154-5.

Sleet Waves (*Élivágar*) : the primordial world of ice; 25, 27-9, 34, 138-9, 186.

Slider (*Sleipnir*) : Odin's horse; 98, 131-2, 151, 153, 188.

Soul Stirrer (*Óðrerir, Óðreyrir*) : one of the three vessels in which the mead Kvasir's Blood is kept; 171, 173, 181.

Spite Cutter (*Níðhǫggr*) : the serpent in Shadow Home that chews the root of Mimir's Wood; 34, see 'Introduction' 18.

Storm Rider (*Hlórriði*) : see '**Thor**'

Strength Field (*Þrúðvangr, Þrúðheimr*) : Thor's realm in Asgarth; 39, 118, 138.

Stumbler (*Svaðilfari*) : the etin builder's horse, father of Slider; 94, 96, 98.

Stumbling Block (*Fallandaforað*) : Hel's threshold; 71.

Sun & Moon (*Sól, Máni*) : sister and brother who drive the sun and moon through the skies; 29-30.

Surt (*Surtr*) : leader of the Sons of Muspell; 186, 189.

Suttung (*Suttungr*) : an etin, Billing's son; 172-4, 177, 179, 181-3, see 'Introduction' 19.

Thanks (*Þǫkk*) : a name taken by Loki in female form, 156; see also '**Loki**'

Thialfi & Roeskva (*Þjálfi, Rǫskva*) : Thor's servants, children of the farmer Egil; 99-100, 102-4, 110-1, 117-8, 135, 137, 142-3, 145.

Thiassi (*Þjazi*) : an etin, father of Skadi; 60-6, 69, see 'Introduction' 19.

Thor (*Þórr*) : a god, champion of the Aesir, known as Storm Rider; 39, 41, 76, 81-3, 85-91, 92, 94, 97, 99-108, 109, 111-8, 119-30, 134-9, 142-6, 151, 157-8, 162-3, 166-8, 188-9, 191.

Thought & Memory (*Huginn, Muninn*) : Odin's ravens; 38.

Thrym (*Þrymr*) : an etin, he steals Thor's Hammer; 86-91.

Thunder Flash (*Bilskirnir*) : Thor's hall; 39, 119.

Thviti (*Þviti*) : the stone used to peg the rock Yell to hold the leash Gleipnir; 75.

Time Farer (*Mundilfœri*) : the father of Sun and Moon; 29.

Tooth Gnasher & Tooth Grinder (*Tanngrísnir, Tanngnjóstr*) : Thor's goats; 39, 83, 88, 99, 136, 142, 151.

Treasure, see 'Jewel & Treasure'

Tyr (*Týr*) : a god, his hand is bitten off by Fenrir; 71, 74-5, 121-3, 129-30, 158, 162, 188.

Unyielding (*Vartari*) : the thong Brokk uses to sew Loki's lips; 84.

Utter Darkness (*Ámsvartnir*) : the lake where Fenrir is bound; 73, 162.

Vali (*Áli, Váli*) : the son of Odin and Rinda, he takes vengeance on Hoder for killing Balder; 179, 191, see 'Introduction' 19-20: for Loki's son Vali, see '**Nari & Vali**'

Valhalla, see 'Kill Hall'

Valkyries, see 'Kill Choosers'

Ve, see 'Vili & Ve'

Vidar (*Viðarr, Víðarr*) : the son of Odin and Grid, he will take vengeance on Fenrir for killing Odin; 142, 158-9, 188, 191.

Vili & Ve (*Vili, Vé*) : Odin's brothers; 27.

War Surge (*Vígríðr*) : the battlefield of the Doom of the Powers; 187.

Warden (*Véurr*) : a name taken by Thor; 121-5; see also 'Thor'

Well of Being (*Urðarbrunnr*) : a well under Asgarth tended by the Norns; 32.

Well of Wisdom (*Mímisbrunnr*) : a well under Etinhome guarded by Mimir; 35-6, 187.

Wide Open (*Víðófnir, Víðópnir*) : the eagle at the top of Mimir's Wood; 32, 34.

Windblown (*Veðrfǫlnir*) : the hawk that sits between Wide Open's eyes; 32.

World Tree, see 'Mimir's Wood'

Yell (*Gjǫll*) : the river at the edge of Shadow Home; 153, see next entry.

Yell (*Gjǫll*) : the rock which holds the leash Gleipnir; 75, see preceding entry.

Yell's Bridge (*Gjallarbrú*) : the bridge over the River Yell; 153-4.

Yeller Horn (*Gjallarhorn*) : Heimdal's horn; 40, 186.

Yelp & Grip (*Gjálp, Greip*) : Geirrod's daughters; 143-5.

Ymir (*Ymir*) : an etin, the first living being; 26-8, 31, 41, 135.

Lightning Source UK Ltd.
Milton Keynes UK
UKOW08f0713160517
301301UK00003B/433/P